THE SCHOOL OF CORE INCOMPETENCE

R. Chandrasekar has worked in both finance and education in the United States and India. His first novel, *The Goat, the Sofa and Mr Swami*, was published by Hachette India in 2010 to very positive reviews.

THE SCHOOL OF CORE INCOMPETENCE

R. Chandrasekar has worked in both finance and education in the United States and India. His first novel, *The Cat, the Stag and Mr Swami* was published by Hachette India in 2010 to very positive reviews.

The School of Core Incompetence

R. Chandrasekar

hachette INDIA

First published in 2012 by Hachette India
(Registered name: Hachette Book Publishing India Pvt. Ltd)
An Hachette UK company
www.hachetteindia.com

SRD

ISBN 978-93-5009-490-7

Hachette Book Publishing India Pvt. Ltd
4th & 5th Floors, Corporate Centre,
Sector 44, Gurgaon 122003, India

Typeset in Dante MT Std 11/13.5
by InoSoft Systems, Noida

Printed and bound in India
by Manipal Technologies Limited, Manipal

MIX
Paper from responsible sources
FSC www.fsc.org FSC™ C043100

For my parents

Understanding your Customer

Corporate Social Responsibility
By Mahender Singh Bhainsla

Corporate Social Responsibility (CSR) is the responsibility of corporate for socialism. As is well known, socialism is one of famous -isms, like capitalism, Marxism and prism. India is home of socialism because of Indiraji and Soniaji and Gandhiji even. So it is very important for corporate to be responsible for socialism. If corporate is not responsible for socialism who will? So CEO big boss like Tata and Ambani and etc need to be responsible for practical socialism so India can help in its progress. Manmohan Singh also emphasizing need for response from corporate hence CSR. Tata and Ambani and all can help in this response so for the spreading of socialism.

There are many types of socialism like Fabian socialism and also others. The Fabian socialists advocated renewal of Western European Renaissance ideas, and their promulgation throughout the rest of the world. The Fabians also favoured the nationalization of land, believing that rents collected by landowners were unearned.

In the period between the two World Wars, the 'Second Generation' Fabians, including the writers R.H. Tawney and Harold Laski, continued to be a major influence on social–democratic thought.

It was at this time that many future leaders of the Third World were exposed to Fabian thought, most notably India's Jawaharlal Nehru (father of Madam Soniaji's mother-in-law). It is a little-known fact that the founder of Pakistan, Barrister Muhammad Ali Jinnah (bad man), was an avid member of the Fabian Society in the early 1930s.

The Fabian and the various other socialism is the responsible of corporate to spread. So it is an important management concept and very important for executive knowledge and so on. Hence it may be stated that CSR is of utmost importance.

Professor Sambandham smoothed out the paper once more and re-read Bhainsla's take on Corporate Social Responsibility.

It was evident that the meat of this literary sandwich was markedly different from the rest. A copy-and-paste job for sure, probably Wikipedia, something he was seeing a lot of since the institute's management decided that providing free internet access was a way of attracting students. And something that, in his mind, strengthened the case for saving himself some trouble by doing away with marks and grades.

He turned the sheet over: an 'A' in red ink in his

familiar hand. The beneficiary of his largesse (and perpetrator of the Fabian fraud) was a member of a large, academically undistinguished contingent from Kurukshetra or Panipat which had made its way down to the Sundarambal Institute of Management, Coimbatore, in search of management excellence.

He looked up reluctantly. Dakshayini – an earnest girl, a regular front-bencher, a pain, one of a group hell-bent on making his life miserable – leaned over with another script. There was no getting away from it. He began to read, trying to look past the 'C' in red ink.

Corporate Social Responsibility
By B. Dakshayini

Companies have a symbiotic relationship with the societies they operate in. They employ people, they use local resources and can also contribute to problems like pollution, overcrowding and traffic issues. While companies are owned by shareholders and need to ensure that shareholders get a good return on the company shares they own, they need to be responsive to the needs of the larger society they operate in.

Corporate Social Responsibility is the umbrella term used to denote ways in which any company can interact in a sustainable way with both people and resources...

He quickly glanced through the rest. Even to his grammatically imperfect eyes it was a well-written, well-argued piece. The ideas looked as though they were couched in words and phrases that were Dakshayini's own. There was cogency to her thoughts and expressions. That 'C' was clearly far short of her due.

He cursed inwardly. That idiot Bhainsla, why couldn't he just accept his good luck and get on with it? Why did he have to share it with all and sundry? And why did he have to share it with Dakshayini of all people? He and his buddies would be sniggering behind Sambandham's back. An avalanche of Fabian sandwich lookalikes with the best Haryanvi antecedents would soon be headed his way and this time he would actually have to wade through the muck and assign proper grades.

Sambandham changed Dakshayini's 'C' to an 'A' and handed her paper back.

'Where did you get this?' he pointed at Bhainsla's paper.

'Sir, one of my friends bought some groundnuts from the shop outside. They came wrapped in this.'

Sambandham was a pot-bellied man of less than medium height with an unruly mop of hair liberally and untidily sprinkled with grey. He saw the world through a pair of thick glasses made partly opaque by a profusion of smudged fingerprints. His clothes were mismatched and had seen better days, and his feet were jammed into sandals whose straps hung loose.

Sundarambal Institute of Management's professor of Business Communications and Management Studies was not all that his title said he was. Peel away the layers that constituted Sambandham's public persona, peel away the dubious diplomas claiming assorted academic achievements and you eventually reached the modest substance of his being: a B.Com. degree. Sambandham had worked his way up from modest beginnings. At a time when a mid-level second class marked the farthest reaches of academic respectability, Sambandham had sweated his way to a middling third. Having learnt little of consequence as a result of his academic exertions and lacking compensatory personal qualities, he got a position as an attendance register clerk in a small college thanks to a kind relative.

Snaking his way home through the traffic on his scooter, Sambandham reflected on the hardscrabble existence of his early days and the struggle to break through to something better. The path from attendance register clerk to professor had been a long and difficult one. There had been times in recent years when he felt he had finally reached a point where he could take a few liberties, where he could take a thing or two for granted.

Like those marks for the CSR paper. Frankly, they were a pain. In his younger, more conscientious days, he had made an effort to actually read the essays that students churned out. He knew that he was as prone to grammaticide as his students and would patiently sit with a copy of Wren and Martin trying to make sense of their grammar and bombast. The ones with poor grades invariably trooped into his office to complain. Nothing short of an improved grade placated them. That would bring in the rest, complaining about grades that were now somehow inadequate.

He tried doing away with grades. The students were willing to live with this but a stern reprimand from AICTE followed by an unhappy session with the director put paid to that experiment.

Backed into a corner, he had entirely given up reading the assignments and settled on distributing grades at random. A fight with his wife meant grief for those unfortunates whose papers were graded afterwards. A sweet smile from his daughter sent grades soaring. Complaints poured in but things were better than in the Wren-and-Martin days since he did not have to waste time reading the assignments. Quick upgrades to anyone who complained worked most of the time and kept the majority somewhat satisfied.

Not wanting to pick further fights with Dakshayini and Co., Sambandham had put off grading their final assignments. He knew the grades were due – he had been officially reminded about them – but he hoped that eventually they would all forget about his grades and find something else to complain about.

Tea at the canteen was one of the few perks the Sundarambal faculty enjoyed. There was a specified time for this, something the habitually dilatory Sambandham ignored. He picked up his cup of tea without acknowledging the waiter behind the counter and sat down at one of the students' tables.

He sipped the tea and made a face. He called the waiter over.

'What is this?' he demanded, pointing at his cup.

'Tea, sir,' replied the unperturbed waiter. He had seen plenty of Sambandham and, after a rough start, had come to realize that the professor didn't really matter and could be safely ignored.

'You call this tea? This is terrible! The previous canteen people served proper tea.'

'You come late and expect us to serve you fresh tea?'

'Don't be cheeky! You should learn to treat faculty with respect.'

The waiter ignored him and walked away with an overt show of indifference. Sambandham glared ineffectually at him and peered once more into his tea. Something caught his eye. He took off his glasses and peered short-sightedly at the table. The waiter was summoned once more. 'What is this?' he asked, pointing at some dried food remnants encrusting the table.

'Don't know, sir,' shrugged the waiter.

'You don't know? This table hasn't been cleaned. These are food stains. This one here looks like dried idli and that looks like dried sambar.'

'If you know, why are you asking me?'

'Why haven't you cleaned this table?'

'Not my job, sir.'

'Not your job? Then whose job is it? Call the in-charge.'

The waiter wandered away desultorily and, an unsatisfactorily long interval later, an older gentleman showed up.

'Yes, professor?'

'These stains. Doesn't anyone clean the tables these days? What are the standards in this place coming to?'

'The tables are cleaned only after all the students are finished. And this is a students' table. The staff table is over there. Why didn't you sit there?'

Sambandham and the canteen boss stared at each other. Sambandham's dirty glasses took the edge off his baleful glare. He shook his head and pointed once more at the offending encrustations. 'Who said the tables should be cleaned only when the students are finished? This is unhygienic. Anytime someone spills something the table should be cleaned.'

'Director's orders,' said the canteen boss, throwing down his trump card with considered insouciance.

'What? What director's orders? Since when has *he* been interested in the canteen tables?'

'Since the committee on green campus submitted its report. It gave recommendations on how to minimize waste. Recommendations were accepted *in toto* by the director and implemented in this canteen as per his orders.' Having delivered this salvo the boss folded his arms, daring any sort of response.

Sambandham swallowed hard. He glanced at his tea – an unappetizing brown wrinkled skin was threatening to hide the liquid from view. A lost cause: Neither his appetite nor his ego had any interest in rapidly cooling tea anymore. But his ego wouldn't let him get up and leave without a last word.

'This is ridiculous,' he spluttered. 'I'm going to see the director about this.' He walked out.

The canteen boss raised his eyebrows, shrugged his shoulders, pushed the chair back in place and walked back to his perch. An interrupted game of Tetris on his mobile awaited him and Sambandham was quickly forgotten.

Organizational Behaviour I

The director had, over the years, become wary of the faculty and other visitors barging in with impossible requests, inconsequential complaints and batty suggestions. A secretary had been installed in the alcove outside to stall visitors and supplicants. The first appointee, a mild-mannered lady named Mrs Malathi Gopalan, had not been up to the task of keeping Sambandham and his colleagues at bay. They had quickly sized her up and figured out that the keys to the sanctum sanctorum lay in a combination of sweet words, outright lies ('the director just called me') and vague insinuations about catastrophes that hung in the air like unexploded time-bombs. They also noticed that she was partial to gossip, and the suggestion that the director's ability to function would be impaired if the latest tidbit did not reach his ears often did the trick when the alternatives failed.

The director was fond of crosswords and disliked being interrupted. Holding on to a thought was becoming more difficult as he aged, and random incursions into his office and thoughts did nothing for the puzzle at hand and little to quell the eruptions of temper that were the invariable outcome of meetings with intruders. Mrs Gopalan was shunted off to the library and a semi-literate but burly man with thick eyebrows and a menacing air was brought in to replace her. The rough exterior concealed an uncomplicated mind. Jagatrakshagan, soon shortened to Jagan, had quickly cottoned on to the fact that the director was the only one who mattered in this corner of the universe, and that periodic explosions of temper from within the sanctum sanctorum did little for his career prospects. Like the canteen head, he had learnt that the faculty could be ignored. He also learnt that certain members of the faculty were not beyond slipping past his desk when he was otherwise occupied. So he had smartly moved his desk to physically obstruct the door to the director's office.

'Jagan, I need to see the director now. Urgent matter.'

Jagan looked up and wondered why he had once held Sambandham and his colleagues in high regard.

'Director is busy, sir. Kindly wait.'

Sambandham scowled, sat down, and pointedly ignored the newspapers and magazines that made the place look like a doctor's or dentist's waiting area. He glared at Jagan to little avail: Jagan knew who the boss was and continued trolling the net for pretty Tamil girls. The new arrangement of furniture suited him perfectly as his surfing activities remained hidden from curious eyes.

Sambandham had grown to like Mrs Gopalan and

had been deeply shocked when Jagan had taken her place. Rough-looking types from the deep south had always made him nervous and he could never shake off the feeling that they made their way through their life (and through his) with a knife or sickle tucked away somewhere. Anti-Brahmin movements over the years had rid Jagan and his ilk of their customary deference. Their loud talk and crude physicality suggested a barely constrained violent streak and Sambandham was always wary of providing the spark that provoked a conflagration.

So he waited, shaking his legs and beating an impatient tattoo on his knees. He avoided eye contact – who knew what Jagan would take as provocation – but looked up surreptitiously every few minutes to see if matters had progressed. As far as he could tell, Jagan was busy on his computer and had not bothered letting the director know he was waiting. Time ticked by.

Sambandham's sense of being put upon, of having been given less than was his due, which had flared up during his exchange with the canteen boss, ebbed. He began to feel a bit foolish. He had noticed the director's increased impatience of late and started to wonder if bringing up the dirty canteen tables was a good idea after all. But, and here was the nub, he had told Jagan that this was an urgent matter, and just getting up and walking away now would make him look rather foolish in Jagan's eyes – a big no-no.

The image of the surly canteen boss, almost mocking in his indifference, passed before him, and the mention of the committee on green campus stirred something within. In the heat of the conversation it hadn't occurred to him that this was the first he was hearing about this committee. A committee had been constituted, had deliberated and come up with recommendations which had been implemented, all without his knowledge. The fires within smouldered, then burst into angry flames.

'Jagan, I am still waiting. I told you it was urgent. Have you told the director?' For the moment, at least, he forgot to worry about the latent violence that Jagan represented.

Jagan looked up. Sweet-looking Thenmozhi from Manamadurai – with fragrant jasmine flowers in her hair – on Tamilmatrimony.com was replaced by Sambandham, smudged glasses and angry scowl thrown in for free. He sighed and, with a show of reluctantly interrupting weighty matters, picked up the phone.

'Prof. Sambandham, sir. No, sir. Yes, sir. About fifteen minutes, sir. He says it is urgent, sir.' Covering the mouthpiece, Jagan looked up. 'Director wants to know why you have been sitting here for fifteen minutes if it is urgent,' he said with a look of bland innocence.

'You… I…' Sambandham spluttered, 'I told you it was urgent… You didn't even tell the director…' He trailed off as he thought he saw Jagan's biceps flex. Damn thugs, uncivilized louts, worming their way into respectable institutions like this one. Ill feelings for Jagan thundered through his thoughts. He wanted to smack Jagan, a couple of sharp cuffs across the ears, a kick on the shin, a bullet through that fat, ugly knee...

'Director will see you in five minutes.' Back to the computer, minimize Thenmozhi, bring up a document... no, not that one. Jagan knew that everyone stole a glance (or two or three) as they edged their way past his desk into the sanctum sanctorum, attempting to glean something of the institute's secrets. For them he had a special page.

Important memo, it began in 36-point, capitalized Times Roman. *For Joint Chancellor's eyes only,* it continued, at a more modest 24 points, but in a bright crimson guaranteed to catch the eye. The large fonts, generous spacing and small screen together meant that the rest of this important information remained off limits for all but the joint chancellor.

Sambandham feigned disinterest as he made his way past Jagan's desk and stole what he thought was a very discreet glance at the computer, something that Jagan was expecting. He winked cheerily at Sambandham and turned back to his monitor. Discomfited and a bit unnerved by the wink, Sambandham walked into the director's room and waited.

Appearances were important for the director and he let Sambandham stew for several long minutes as he squinted at his laptop screen and typed something seemingly important. He sported a frown that he hoped was indicative of deep thinking and concentrated immersion in unravelling some complex skeins of management thought. He nodded a few times as though reaching some conclusion, tapped away some more before looking up and affecting mild surprise at Sambandham's presence.

'Ah, Professor Sambandham. Do sit down.'

Sambandham sat leaning forward, resting his elbows on the director's desk.

'Yes?' inquired the director. Having acknowledged Sambandham's presence, he turned his attention back to his laptop.

'Sir, I have been a faculty here for over ten years,' began Sambandham. The depth of his grievance needed to be conveyed and some historical background would lay the foundation for a detailed and pointed account of his concerns. 'First in Commerce, then in Management. In all that time I have only had the institute's well-being first and foremost in mind. I have sacrificed my personal time, taking extra classes even, only for the growth and prosperity of the institute. And various activities, extra-curricular activities as well. When help and advice was sought for, I have used my rich personal experience to provide guidance and direction. My advice on these various matters has always been well appreciated.'

He paused for effect. The director's attention was still on the laptop and he was nodding slowly. Sambandham took this as agreement and ploughed on.

'I have been thinking about many aspects of this institute's functioning from the management perspective. I have always suggested thoughts, improvements even, for the betterment of the functioning and better utilization of the scarce resources that this institution has at its disposal. And now, I'm sorry to say, things are happening behind my back. Committees are being formed, important committees even, and not only am I not told about it but my respected opinion and advice is also not being sought.'

He paused once more, expecting the director to express concern and ask for further details. No such concern was expressed; the director was implacable in his devotion to his laptop. Sambandham's flood of words faltered.

'Sir, please…'

A nod, a brief moment of eye contact.

'This committee on green campus… It has been constituted, deliberations have occurred, even recommendations have been made. My understanding is that implementations have also started. Just today I have learnt that in the cafeteria the tables are not to be wiped until all the students have finished spilling all their things… Why was my advice not sought, sir?'

'Ah, yes, yes. And what were you saying, professor?'

Sambandham swallowed hard. He had started with the background, stated his case and moved smoothly to the particular point that concerned him. All following the template he had set out for his class. It hadn't worked. The bloody director had not been paying attention. He started again, hesitation and doubts fracturing the flow of words.

'Hmm,' said the director, still staring intently at his laptop. 'How are your classes progressing, professor?'

'Sir, the students are appreciating my approach. They like the practical touches that I am providing. I am using my rich practical experience to provide guidance and direction in the field of management communications and this the students have greatly appreciated. But this committee on green campus…'

'You have been giving the students adequate feedback on their performance?'

'But of course, sir. That is my bounden duty which I am following as per guidelines…'

'Professor Sambandham,' the director looked up and spoke briskly, 'I have been told that the final marks from your Communications class have not been submitted and are now overdue by…' he made a show of consulting a calendar, 'more than two weeks. You have been sent two reminders already. Without your marks the students' grade sheets cannot be finalized. Without those grade sheets the placement communications to companies cannot start. Your concern for the institute and its students is commendable. But you can demonstrate this concern better by submitting your marks on time.'

Sambandham reeled under this unexpected flanking attack.

'Sir, preparing detailed evaluation of each student's communications portfolio is time-consuming and…'

'Precisely the reason I have not burdened you with responsibilities on the green committee. So, may we expect your marks by, say, Friday?'

Two days away and, damn, he hadn't even started. And this was as close to an order with a gun held to his head that he was likely to get.

'Okay, sir, yes, sir,' he said weakly and got up to leave.

'Oh, just one more thing.'

He blanched.

'Since you are so keen on sharing your…umm… expertise and experience in administrative matters, there *is* something you can help with. But only after the registrar confirms receipt of those marks.'

The director turned back to his laptop, this time with a distinct sense of finality. Aware that he had been dismissed, Sambandham shuffled out.

Interpreting Regulations

The Director,
Sundarambal Institute of Management,
Peelamedu,
Coimbatore

Sir,

Ref: Visit of Official Evaluation Committee from AICTE to Sundarambal Institute of Management, Coimbatore, on 20th March 2011

Please find summary findings of the above mentioned Committee to your institution enclosed herewith.

1. The overall evaluation was SATISFACTORY subject to the observations detailed below. The lacunae observed may kindly be rectified at the earliest instance.
2. The number of courses and total contact hours fall short of norms. AICTE norms call for a minimum of 1440 (one thousand four hundred and forty) contact

hours for the MBA programme. It was observed that your institution's MBA programme structure includes only 1426 (one thousand four hundred and twenty six) approved contact hours. The shortfall may kindly be rectified at the earliest.

3. The number of departments and faculty therein were as per norms.
4. The quantum of books and periodicals in the library was VERIFIED.
5. Committee questioned the necessity for maintaining a large lawn. It was pointed out by the Committee that substantial savings of water as well as emoluments paid to the gardener could be effected by converting the lawn into a dry garden. The services of a landscape architect are recommended thereto.
6. The Committee noted a shortfall (13 numbers) in the number of dustbins. AICTE norms call for 1 dustbin (plastic, with lid) of 3600cc capacity for every 10 students. The same may kindly be rectified before the next evaluation.
7. The Committee noted that the ladies WC (second floor, B Block) had a men's urinal attached to the north wall. It was observed by the Committee that lady students and faculty availing this facility may be put to significant inconvenience as a result. The services of a competent plumber are recommended to rectify the same.
8. The number of fans in the classrooms was as per norms.

9. The Committee noted the presence of 2 (two) rats in the canteen in violation of norms. AICTE norms (as amended vide circular number 2263/44/07) call for elimination of rats using humane means so as not to distress the learning process in academic institutions. The said lacuna may kindly be rectified using the services of an AICTE-certified rat catcher at the earliest. Regional offices of AICTE maintain a list of AICTE-certified rat catchers and the same may be availed of.
10. The Committee noted that the titles of the courses were not as per norms. Appendix 1 (attached) lists violations of AICTE course title norms. The Committee observed that confusion among the students might prevail as a result. The same may be rectified at the earliest.
11. In view of the shortfalls in meeting norms as observed thereof, the Committee's recommendation is that the overall evaluation of SATISFACTORY be maintained subject to the evaluation of a Surprise Inspection Committee (SIC) within the next three months. Particular weight will be given to those areas where lacunae have been observed. It may be noted that continued violation of norms may result in withdrawal of recognition or a fine of Rs 500 (five hundred only).

Yours sincerely,
A.P. Gupta
Secretary to the Committee

The letter had been folded and refolded. A number of rubber stamps confirmed both its authenticity and its receipt by the Sundarambal office. A series of initials attested to its progress through the Sundarambal bureaucracy.

The director stared at his laptop. Sambandham, seated across him, stared at the letter. His thinking done with, the director looked up at Sambandham. 'In view of your rich experiences in dealing with various institute-related matters, and your relative efficiency in the submission of the final marks, I am entrusting you with the task of removing the lacunae pointed out by the committee.'

Sambandham looked apprehensive. This had all the makings of a cleverly laid trap and he wished that he had not brought up the business of the green committee the previous week.

'I shall endeavour to give full satisfaction, sir,' he began. 'I will henceforth institute a study to investigate the modalities of complying with said lacunae at the earliest.'

'Professor,' interjected the director, 'we don't have the time to look into modalities. I am looking for concrete steps, for quick action. The surprise inspection committee is expected on 15 May and everything should be complete by then.'

'Sir,' stammered Sambandham, 'how do you know when the surprise inspection committee is coming? Isn't it meant to be a surprise?'

'As per the norms, AICTE is required to give one month's notice before a surprise inspection.'

'Sir?'

'You see, there was a time when a surprise inspection was just that. For institutions that didn't have a source within AICTE, that is. They discovered, on one of their genuine surprise visits, that five colleges in Allahabad were sharing faculty and their library.'

'I don't understand, sir. How could they share their library?'

'The book racks had wheels. They would just wheel the racks onto a tempo and take them to the next college. Got caught red-handed and their recognition was withdrawn. Went to court alleging that they were denied due process, their constitutional right to privacy violated, and the raid demonstrated mala fide intentions on AICTE's part. The court agreed and said that proper notice of surprise inspections needed to be given. The expert committee constituted by AICTE to study the court's order and come up with recommendations suggested one month as appropriate notice for a surprise inspection. Regular inspections require three months' notice.'

Sambandham looked at the letter and the said lacunae.

'Sir, last time they came they complained about less numbers of ladies' bathrooms. We rectified that by converting the men's bathroom and now they are complaining about the presence of a urinal there.'

'It is their job to discover lacunae. If they go back with none, they might find themselves without a job. But make sure they don't discover the same lacunae.'

'This Appendix 1. Last time they said that the course

title "Communications" was not as per norms and suggested "Business Communications". Now they are saying even this is not as per norms and are suggesting "Business and Management Communications". How many times am I to change this? Students are getting confused and are even complaining.'

'The exigencies of keeping up with developments. We are in a post-dotcom, post-9/11, post-Lehman world. AICTE is only fulfilling its mandate to keep syllabi updated.'

As happened many times when conversing with the director, Sambandham felt the full weight of his inadequate education. The word exigency sounded important, but he didn't know what it meant. He wasn't entirely sure what the post-dotcom, post-9/11 and post-Lehman world was, though the terms themselves were vaguely familiar. What he did know was that he had to change the titles of his courses when asked to, but that no one seemed concerned with the contents of his courses. These stayed static in the face of the changing world, exigencies or no exigencies.

'So, professor, I'm sure you can do the needful. I know the institute can depend on you.'

'Sir, there are so many things. Rats, toilets, dustbins, courses even. I also have two courses to teach.'

'I have made sure you have help. I've constituted an AICTE review committee. You are the chairman, of course, reporting directly to me. I am including professors Thilakavathi, Agarwal, Anbuchezian and Nilakantan in the committee. They will assist you. You can give me weekly updates. Remember we need to have everything in place at least a week before 15 May.'

'How does that man expect me to work with them?'

Used to her husband's daily grumbling, Mrs Sambandham ignored him and carried on with her cooking.

'Don't just ignore me. Listen. That director has made me chairman of a committee.'

She looked up for a moment. He wasn't the sort to pull her leg. Their interactions rarely deviated from mundane and quotidian matters and humour was entirely absent in their marriage. He didn't look drunk either. It was a bit odd but maybe work pressures were getting to him. Still, that wasn't her headache. Her job was to keep the house clean and keep everyone in it fed. His office problems were not her concern. She continued to ignore him.

'I'm telling you, woman, that director has made me chairman of the AICTE review committee.'

They had married when he was still an attendance clerk. Theirs had been an arranged marriage with a large enough number of go-betweens to ensure that neither family had a clue about the other. Small exaggerations and the odd white lie had made their way up and down the chain as the intermediaries sought to hurry matters to a satisfactory conclusion. The result was a distinct falling of scales when Sambandham and his wife finally met on the day of their wedding.

While Sambandham resigned himself to make do with what he had got, his wife never got over the feeling that she had been had. Over the years he made his way out of the clerical morass and onto the ladder of academic respectability. He remained a clerk to her, though, and when he came home with news of progress and promotions, she automatically added them to the list of lies and exaggerations that formed the bedrock of their marriage. Hence her complete lack of empathy or sympathy about his chairmanship of the dysfunctional committee.

Conducting a Meeting

Sambandham had put in some effort to write down his opening remarks, in which he tried to incorporate some of the principles covered in his Communications course. There was an introduction, a statement of problems, suggestions and a conclusion. Wren and Martin had been consulted, some lines of argument had been drawn up, and some tentative work plans suggested. After some thought, he decided not to conclude the meeting with the national anthem.

He knew there were sensitivities involved and wanted to avoid a situation where they ended up at complete cross-purposes. Hovering over his thoughts was the knowledge that the director would quite happily let him hang if things went wrong.

Things started going downhill even before he was done clearing his throat. His colleagues, never ones to let an agenda guide their discussions, jumped the gun.

Professor Thilakavathi was first off the mark, as always. 'Why are we wasting time on this nonsense?'

Thilakavathi was a feisty lady who made it a point to get to the point without much ado. Her colleagues had difficulty imagining her as anyone's wife. She had a son, which implied that there was a spouse somewhere in the picture. Campus gossip had it that Mr Thilakavathi had found refuge in the Middle East, buying peace and harmony with a substantial monthly contribution to the family exchequer.

'The director has asked us to...'

'Who is the director to ask us?'

Silence.

'We have been asked to look into the ladies' bathroom, I see,' said Professor Nilakantan, peering at his copy of the letter. 'As gentlemen, we are not in a position to enter the ladies' bathroom, let alone look at what goes on in there. We are therefore unable to supervise the correction of this alleged lacuna. Therefore this responsibility should be entrusted to Professor Thilakavathi, I feel.'

Professor Thilakavathi glared at him.

'Are you suggesting, Professor Nilakantan, that I am here to look after the bathrooms? Do I look like a bathroom cleaner to you? You can bloody well look after the bathrooms yourself.'

'You Brahmins think you are too superior to clean the bathrooms. Mind you, those days are long past!' Professor Anbuchezian had stood up and was now shouting even as he wagged a finger at Nilakantan. 'Today justice has been done, social justice. You can go and clean your own shit!'

'Damn right!' shouted Thilakavathi.

Nilakantan went blood red and had difficulty getting his words out.

'You...you...you monkey. You buffalo. No better than monkeys or buffaloes you all are. Professor Sambandham, I formally propose that professors Anbuchezian and Thilakavathi be assigned the task of seeing that the lacuna in the ladies' bathroom pointed out in the AICTE report is removed.'

'Who is responsible for minuting this meeting?' inquired Professor Agarwal.

'We are being insulted by this creature here and you are asking about minutes?' thundered Thilakavathi. 'Don't you North Indians have anything better to do?'

'Please, please, please... Kindly calm down. I appeal...kindly calm down,' begged Sambandham.

'Arre, all meetings I am attending we have minutes. Important for AICTE and so forth and also for providing a record of our deliberations. But you Madrasis are always fighting about caste and suchlike matters. Cannot be minuted obviously.'

'How dare you refer to us as Madrasis? You Hindiwalas think that any South Indian is a Madrasi. Professor Sambandham, I demand an apology, else I shall be constrained to resign from the committee.'

'Please, please, please...'

'Arre, why are you getting so upset, Thilakavathi madam?'

'I am not a madam, I'm a professor.'

'Professor, why are you getting upset? No insult or anything intended.'

'I'm not a Madrasi. In fact, there is no city called Madras anymore. How can I, or anyone else for that matter, be a Madrasi?'

'Our respected and beloved leader, Dr Kalaignar Karunanidhi, delivered a great present to the Tamil people and renamed said city Chennai,' chimed in Anbuchezian.

'Leader? What leader? He leads only people like you,' spat out Nilakantan. 'Now my proposal…'

'First he calls me monkey, then he calls me a buffalo, then he insults our leader. You brahmins are like dead dogs now…'

'Shut up, all of you!'

Agarwal had stood up and was glaring at all of them. There was a stunned silence. He had anticipated a calmer, more contemplative atmosphere when he had moved south and had yet to reconcile himself to the hot-tempered eruptions that marked faculty meetings. The physicality of the north was absent here, but the physical settling of scores also meant a settled hierarchy and a clear sense of one's place in the overall scheme of things. Here things were fluid and one was never sure when the ground would shift beneath one's feet.

'Why are we fighting like this? The director has constituted this committee and asked us to consider many important matters. Has he provided snacks for us while we toil? A glass of water even?'

They looked at each other and then at Agarwal. He nodded meaningfully before sitting down and continuing.

'In the north, we are worried about our rights. If we don't insist, people take advantage. Here we have so many responsibilities: teaching, students, committees and so on. But not so much concern about our rights. So what I am saying is, if the director wants us to exercise our responsibilities, some tea, coffee, snacks and so on and so forth will assist us in the discharge of these responsibilities. After all, the efficient discharge of our responsibilities is in the best interests of the institute.'

He had their undivided attention now. Even Nilakantan and Anbuchezian's blood feud was in abeyance for the moment.

'So I am suggesting, the first thing we should do is minute our request.'

Nods of agreement, vehement assent even.

'Which is why I am asking who is responsible for the minutes, so we can officially convey the decisions of this learned committee to the director.'

Wary looks went all around. Minuting the official decisions of the committee and conveying the same to the director was something each of them wanted to take a pass on. As though by telepathy, the wandering looks converged and, as Sambandham somehow sensed they would, settled on him.

'Since the director has appointed you chairman of this committee, might I propose that you minute the proceedings of this meeting,' said Thilakavathi, looking at Sambandham.

'Seconded,' added Agarwal.

'Yes, yes,' mumbled Anbuchezian and Nilakantan, abashed at finding themselves in agreement on something.

Sambandham waited for some voice of moderation or dissent, some suggestion that responsibility might be shared, but in vain.

'Okay, okay,' he sighed, 'I shall record that the majority of the committee requested tea and coffee.'

'Majority?' inquired Thilakavathi. 'Is this not unanimous?'

Four vigorous nods.

Unwilling to appear to break faculty solidarity and terrified at the thought of conveying the committee's demands to the director, Sambandham wished he was elsewhere, doing something else, even correcting those damned Communications – sorry, Business and Managerial Communications – papers. Outnumbered four to one, he nodded weakly.

Anbuchezian was unwilling to leave it at that. He was ever ready to dig up a grievance and any suggestion that social justice was not being served constituted a grievance in his eyes.

'We are demanding, not requesting,' he shouted. 'Unanimous demanding. None of this requesting nonsense. Demanding our rights only as Periyar would have said.'

'Yes, he is right,' chimed in Thilakavathi.

'Perhaps along with tea and coffee we can also have idli and vadai,' piped up Nilakantan.

Anbuchezian thought for a moment of protesting that idli and vadai were Brahmin dishes, then remembered that he liked them as much as any Brahmin.

'Arre, idli and all are very nice, but we can also have kachoris and samosas.'

'Why not, why not?'

'Professor Sambandham, kindly include all this in the minutes.'

Sambandham, preoccupied by the impending meeting with the director, outflanked and outnumbered by his fellow committee members, could only scribble away in his notebook.

Nilakantan, who had been going through the AICTE letter with a furrowed brow, added to Sambandham's misery. 'It says here that AICTE has noted the presence of two numbers of rats in the canteen.'

'So what?' countered Thilakavathi. 'We don't need AICTE to tell us this. I could have told you that myself. Are you now going to suggest that Anbuchezian and I eliminate the rats as well?'

Nilakantan loathed Anbuchezian and Thilakavathi and would gladly have assigned them the task of catching the rats. Not now, though. They had somehow contrived to put that incompetent fool Sambandham on the spot and the time was right to put the screws on him. There was enough time to deal with the two of them later.

'Of course not,' he said in as ingratiating a tone as he could muster. 'I merely felt that in view of the presence of the rats which has been duly noted by you in addition to the AICTE representatives, it might be better if the tea and coffee and idli and vadai and samosas and kachoris were provided by an outside vendor rather than our canteen.'

This was met with ready acquiescence on Agarwal's part, agreement with some studied reluctance on the part of Thilakavathi and Anbuchezian, and morose neutrality from Sambandham. He was as ready as the rest to partake of food from Saravana Bhavan or elsewhere, but the landscape of his meeting with the director was turning more difficult with every additional suggestion from these blasted colleagues of his.

'Kindly note all this in the minutes as well.'

Having exhausted themselves of emotions, insults and suggestions, the committee let the meeting meander to a desultory close. There was some discussion of likely suppliers of snacks, suggestions that this important decision not be left to the director's discretion, and general agreement that the date of the next meeting be left hanging pending the director's action on the (minuted) suggestions of the committee. Vague threats of action should the director ignore the committee's suggestions were also left floating in the air. Well pleased with the outcome, the committee dispersed, with Sambandham left to carry the can.

This was the outcome he had feared, and reflecting on the proceedings as he trudged back to his room he had the distinct sense that things were even worse than he had anticipated. Postponing the writing of the minutes was not an option: both the director and his committee colleagues would expect him to do something before the surprise inspection took place.

Organization Theory

To most in the institute, the director was at the pinnacle, both in terms of being the boss and in terms of that more ephemeral quality: status. The director himself knew better; he was aware of the organizational layers above him in the broader Sundarambal hierarchy, layers that were both a mental and physical burden. And, like any self-respecting member of a hierarchical organization, he made sure that those below him were aware of *his* status. He knew that status was hard earned and that losing it took only a moment's carelessness.

So he barricaded himself behind Jagan and the firmly closed doors. His public appearances were carefully orchestrated. He taught only the absolute freshers. Their callowness and receptive minds with thoughts unsullied by the shallowness of the academic journey they were on, their eagerness to lap up his tales of corporate intrigues and achievements and their quick laughter at his well worn jokes all served as a tonic to his self-esteem and added to his aura. All of which was necessary because he was acutely aware of the gap between image and reality. The director lived in fear of being caught with his pants down.

Reality meant waiting in a well-worn chair while being ignored by the joint chancellor's secretary. The secretary and the joint chancellor represented two of the layers that oppressed him. As his title indicated, the joint chancellor himself was a mere stepping stone to the rarefied and exalted layers that marked the highest reaches of the Sundarambal empire.

The director hoped no one from his institute would see him, beads of sweat and fidgety hands betraying his nervousness, his stiff back and alert mien marking him out as a supplicant.

'Ah, Thiru director, sit down, sit down.'

The director attempted to maintain a fine balance between looking too eager and being too relaxed. He sat a few inches back from the edge of his chair to retain some of his dignity, and a few inches ahead of the backrest to convey careful attention and the right measure of respect.

The joint chancellor leaned back in his well-upholstered chair and cracked his heavily ringed fingers with the look of a man who knew he was the boss. After all, he was the chancellor's nephew.

The chancellor himself was based in distant Chennai and this campus was just one tendril in a vast forest of business ventures. As with his other commercial enterprises, he had appointed a relative with a mandate to keep the business running satisfactorily. The joint chancellor – the title a nod to the academic veneer of this enterprise – had to ensure that the enterprise delivered its revenue with a minimum burden on the exchequer. Academics were not his thing: neither the practice nor the practitioners were worthy of his time or interest. He felt that they were a bunch of gas-bags and losers, and in darker moments cursed his uncle for dumping him in this backwater. Those who interacted with him, the director included, were made fully aware of his condescension and disinterest.

'Director, last year you were unable to fill all your seats.'

The director moistened his lips and shifted uneasily in his chair.

'Yes, sir, but I must plead extenuating circumstances. There were 250 seats available and we received only 321 applications. We have to follow AICTE guidelines and so had to reject 23 applicants whose undergraduate marks were below the norms. It would have created the wrong impression if we had given admissions without even an interview. We needed to build up the image of the institute as you are well aware. Going through the motions of an interview is essential in my opinion, but only 204 appeared for the interview and...'

The joint chancellor had transferred his attention to his iPhone while the director was making his point and now looked up.

'That is all very nice but I must emphasize that seats are there to be filled. How many seats are there in Parliament?'

'Sir?'

'Are you deaf? I am asking one simple question. How many seats are there in Parliament?'

'The Lok Sabha has 500-odd seats…'

'And how many of them are empty?'

'I'm not too sure…'

'Zero! Zero is the correct answer. If they can fill 500 seats in Parliament, why can't you fill 250 in your institute?'

'We are making all efforts…'

The joint chancellor cut him short. 'See chancellor there,' he gestured at an overwhelmingly large photograph of an indeterminately middle-aged gentleman. The chancellor sported a thick black mane of slicked-back hair, a ferocious and well-groomed moustache, a spotless white shirt and a beatific air that somehow conveyed menace. He was a familiar presence around the campus. That photograph graced all the rooms in the campus, except for the toilets. Actual sightings were rare, though. Like the summit of a tall mountain that remains obscured by clouds, fleeting glimpses were all that the chancellor allowed lesser mortals.

'Chancellor has devoted his life to social service. Providing worthy education to the people. More people getting educated, more the benefits to society – and that is chancellor's desire. So I am repeating for your benefit. All seats must be filled. Like Parliament. After all, if seats in Parliament are not filled, how can they serve the people?'

Students don't exactly grow on trees, the director thought to himself. They are not exactly thick on the ground. Well, that might not be entirely correct – but he had trawled the length and width of the country, large swathes of it anyway, attempting to persuade them to come to this hardscrabble stretch of land near Coimbatore. It was a hard business, a humiliating business, something that kept him away for days on end from his fortress-like, comfortable and air-conditioned office. Last year, he had scraped together a class of 179. Word of mouth was important when it came to repeat business and word would surely have got out about the quality of education on offer at Sundarambal. How on earth was he going to net 250 this time around? He broke out in a sweat despite the super-cooled air.

'We are requesting AICTE for 125 additional seats,' the joint chancellor went on inexorably. The director's mouth fell open. 'I understand that AICTE committee is coming for inspection soon. They are creating some difficulty with these additional seats. Why, I don't know. Perhaps negotiations are called for. So you please handle negotiations with the visiting committee. We must have 375 seats next year and once again I am emphasizing that all seats must be filled.'

How the hell did the joint chancellor know that an AICTE committee was coming? And how was the director supposed to bring in 375 students? And he had thought that academia, even the diluted offerings that passed for academia in this place, would be a refuge from the cut-throat corporate grind with its culture of unattainable targets.

'Negotiations...'

'Yes. Chancellor is of the opinion that 375 is a good number for the management programme. We have put in our request. Now you make sure to fulfil chancellor's desires by negotiating with AICTE.'

The director shook his head as he walked back to his office. The joint chancellor's interest in AICTE and the expansion of seats was completely out of character. In fact, the blighter had never expressed an interest in anything other than money and girls. How was the director going to fill those bloody seats, and how was he going to negotiate with those AICTE bastards? Disturbing and discomfiting thoughts weighed down on him as he walked past the monumental buildings representing the chancellor's devotion to social service.

Information Flow in Organizations

Professor Nallakannu knocked on the door and walked in without waiting for a formal welcome. Thilakavathi looked up, annoyed. She had been trolling the net for her 10-year-old son's school project: a PowerPoint presentation on nanotechnology. The Indian cricket team was playing a tournament, and that, coupled with his daily excursions into neighbouring streets for gully cricket sessions, meant that the deadline for the presentation had neared without the boy being any the wiser about nanotechnology. And so, along with fellow parents, she was engaged in a last ditch effort to save junior's backside.

All of this, clearly, was not for Nallakannu's eyes. Knowing this, he took a casual detour around the office to try and catch a glimpse of what she was up to. Knowing him, she turned the monitor away. He was used to these little games and took failure in his cheerful stride.

'You look very busy, Professor Thilaka,' he said, making himself comfortable.

'Trying to complete my research paper,' she frowned, keeping her eyes on the screen.

Nallakannu was not put off by the lack of eye contact. 'Yes, we need to keep up with the developments. Myself, I shall be attending a conference in Madurai next month.' He paused, waiting for her to ask him about the conference, about whether the institute was funding his attendance (it was), whether he was travelling by second-class AC (he was), or whether he had cleverly arranged things to make a long weekend of it (he had). She didn't oblige, making a point of keeping an unwavering eye on her screen.

'So...your research paper, what might be the subject matter if I may ask?'

You may bloody well not ask, she thought venomously. But she knew there was no getting away from him. 'Marketing implications of nanotechnology,' she said.

'Oh,' he said, impressed despite himself. He had assumed she was surfing the web on the institute's time. 'And, according to your research, what are the marketing implications of nanotechnology?'

'That is what I was trying to work out when you walked in.'

'I am disturbing you then?'

She knew he wasn't going to leave anytime soon despite his protestations. Besides, there was this rising froth of resentment at having to save her dilatory son's butt. She needed a break from nanotechnology. With a show of reluctance at having to tear herself away from her work, she beat out some final words on the keyboard and looked up.

'Did you know, Nallakannu sir, that nanotechnology calls for a new paradigm? The four Ps are inadequate to deal with evolving technologies. Utterly inadequate. I'm trying to think of eight Qs and sixteen Rs to fill the gaps. But it is tough. That Prahlad fellow has already taken "Bottom of the Pyramid". Ditto "Small is Beautiful". So new buzzwords which define the nano paradigm are needed.'

None of this made any sense to Nallakannu. He taught statistics and the finer points of management jargon were lost on him.

'Interesting. Very interesting. All of this has implications, I'm sure. Paradigms and implications. Managerial paradigms and implications, that is. But with the director asking you to be on the AICTE committee and all, you must be finding it very difficult to research all these paradigms. Your time is being taken up with committee-related work, no?'

'Oh, that director! Does he ask us before dumping committee work on us? No. He takes us completely for granted. Here I am researching new marketing paradigms for the post-dotcom nanotech world with a special emphasis on bio-related nano management paradigms, deep in thought on developing concepts with the potential to put this institute on the cutting edge of management thought and he forms this committee to deal with that urinal in the ladies' bathroom.'

'Urinal in ladies' bathroom?'

'Yes. You know that bathroom on the second floor of B block which they converted into a ladies' facility after the last AICTE visit? They didn't remove the men's urinal.'

Nallakannu leaned forward and spoke conspiratorially. 'That Nilakantan. He uses that bathroom sometimes. I have seen him with my own eyes.'

'What? That bastard Nilakantan had the effrontery to suggest that I be put in charge of removing that urinal! Nallakannu sir, you tell me if that is fair. I am forced to interrupt paradigm-changing management thinking while that Brahmin idiot Nilakantan spends his time peeing in the ladies' loo.'

'Not good, Professor Thilaka. You are a great paradigm thinker and what you are being asked to do is not good. Now I have also interrupted you and your thinking, so I will also be going.' Shutting the door quietly behind him, he exited.

Distracted, upset at having been reminded yet again of her committee responsibilities, she returned once more to her computer. Academic enterprise on her son's behalf gave way to lethargy and a desire to get the damned thing over with. Summoning up the Wikipedia article on nanotechnology, she cut and pasted with savage gusto.

She had thrown words and jargon at Nallakannu. On second thought, though, perhaps she could make something of that meaningless jumble of words and jargon. Some work, some alliterative buzzwords that could substitute for thought, and there just might be enough for an article. There might even be a paradigm or two just waiting to be unearthed. Perhaps she could present some of this at a conference. That Nallakannu had mentioned something about one. If that idiot could present a paper, so could she. She had been here long enough to deserve a paid trip; she would have to corner him sometime and find out just what he had been able to wangle.

Nilakantan had ten siblings – six brothers and four sisters. As the eighth child, he had grown up in a household where the joy attending each new arrival had faded into a resigned acceptance of fate. His had been an upbringing by default. His father had discovered him running around the house aimlessly one day when he was eight and was surprised to learn that no one had remembered to get him admitted to school. An elder sibling had then been entrusted with the task. That done, no one remembered to keep track of his progress in school, which was probably just as well given his inability to make a mark in anything. He came of age at a time where reservations had closed off most options for underachieving upper-caste sorts and, as a charter member of that tribe, he felt the consequences more than most.

Several of his siblings had shrugged off these inconveniences and prospered. But not Nilakantan. Despite the pride he felt at the achievements of his siblings and the larger Brahmin community, he carried within him a deep sense of inadequacy and a cancerous hatred of the system (and its practitioners) which had deposited him (and others like him) in a cul-de-sac without hope.

He was clear-headed enough to see the institute, his colleagues and his students for what they were, and while one part of him grudgingly accepted his presence in this company, a larger part could not contain his resentment at the broader circumstances that had landed him there. Teaching was something he had ended up in following aborted trysts with other professions. He did not have an aptitude for it and lived in dread of being cornered in the classroom with questions to which he had no answers. Over time, he had worked out a method that kept him at a certain distance from classroom discussions and inconvenient questions, a method that he continued to practise with every batch of students, like the current one.

'Take dictation,' Nilakantan shouted, as he paced back and forth with a well-worn sheaf of notes. 'Contingent Liabilities. Contingent liabilities have been defined by the Institute – capital I – of Chartered – capital C – Accountants – capital A – of India – capital I – as liabilities which are contingent in nature.'

'Sir, how do you spell contingent?'

He spelt it out in a rhythmic monotone much like the ticking of a clock – a deliberate cadence perfected by years of experience. This allowed him to stretch his limited source material and had the added benefit of lulling the bulk of the students into a state of near catatonia.

'Examples of contingent liabilities include...'

'Sir, what exactly is the meaning of contingent in the context of corporate actions?'

He looked up, upset at this interruption.

'Who is asking?'

'Sir, me, sir.' It was that pestilential Dakshayini. Why had she landed here and not in one of the IIMs was a mystery neither he nor any of his colleagues had been able to fathom. 'Also, could you tell us if the contracts written by Bear Stearns pre-2008 were contingent liabilities on their books?'

'Miss Dakshayini, if you had been listening to the dictation, you would have noticed that I was about to give examples of contingent liabilities. But you are already interrupting before I give you this important information.'

'Sir, sorry, sir, but...'

'No buts.' He looked at the rest of the class. 'Shall I answer Miss Dakshayini's question or shall I continue to give information which will be appearing in your exam?'

The Kurukshetra and Panipat lot were adamant in their preference for examination-related enlightenment, the rest were passive in their indifference, and a distraught Dakshayini found herself alone in wanting to know more about Bear Stearns's pre-2008 contingent liabilities.

'Okay, then, take dictation.' He looked around to make sure everyone was taking dictation. 'Examples of contingent liabilities include...'

Some forty minutes later, an electric bell allowed Nilankantan to stop mid-sentence amidst a general shuffling of papers, books and the assorted detritus that accompanies the twenty-first-century management student into the classroom.

Dakshayini intercepted him before he could make his way out.

'Sir, I know it is not part of the syllabus and I am sorry to have interrupted your lecture but I have been reading about the role of contingent liabilities in precipitating the financial crisis of 2008 and am curious to know whether the derivative contracts written by them constitute contingent liabilities. Could you help me?'

Shit. How could he get rid of her without exposing his ignorance of Bear Stearns and their bloody contingent liabilities?

'You see, it is a complicated question. So complicated that several committees have been constituted to look at this very question. Many policies, decisions and strategies depend on the answer, which is why so much effort and time is being spent to getting to the bottom of this. The problem is, how exactly do you define contingent liabilities in the context of a company like Bear Stearns? First you have to properly classify and categorize Bear Stearns. If you don't do that you are liable to get incorrect answers. Second is the question of which liability exactly is contingent. This question is also troubling various committees even as we speak. So, without knowing the outcome of the deliberations of the committees constituted thereto, the answer to your question must remain in abeyance.' In the course of his professional meanderings Nilakantan had spent time as a bureaucrat and the stonewalling skills he had learnt there had proved useful in subsequent careers, including this one.

Stunned by this unexpected eloquence from the otherwise deadly dull 'Take Dictation', Dakshayini could only mutter a weak, 'Thank you, sir. So sorry for interrupting. I hadn't realized it was such a complicated issue,' before following her classmates out.

Pleased with himself, Nilakantan wandered back to his room and was somewhat surprised to find Nallakannu loitering with intent in the corridor outside.

'Just a few minutes of your time, professor.' Nallakannu could be ingratiating when he chose to. He knew his victims well and chose his approach carefully. 'Coming from class?'

'Yes, yes, first year class. I was clearing up some technical points on contingent liabilities after class. Some of these youngsters are keen on furthering their knowledge and your humble self is always keen on obliging.'

'So you are not giving dictation anymore?' Nilakantan's teaching methods were no secret.

'What? Oh. No, no. Dictation is for essential facts. It is a tried and trusted method, believe me, and students appreciate the clarity. But I discuss the finer points. After all, our director is always pushing for an active learning process as opposed to a passive learning process. Like planting seeds instead of scattering weeds. Hence this technical clarification on contingent liabilities.'

'Technically, what is a contingent liability? Begging your pardon, but I ask as a mere statistician looking to further his knowledge.'

'Ah, that is a very complicated matter as I was telling the students. You see, sometimes liabilities are contingent and sometimes not. Sometimes contingencies are liabilities and sometimes not. It all depends. The context of the question is all-important. The question that was raised was in the context of Bear Stearns.'

'Bear Stearns?'

'Yes, Bear Stearns.'

'If I may ask, what is Bear Stearns?'

'Ah, now that is the complication. You have gone to the heart of the issue, Professor Nallakannu. You see, several committees have been constituted to answer that very question, particularly in the context of contingent liability which itself is a very vexed subject. It is a very deep matter which is a challenge to clarify particularly in the context of first year students. But we have to try. Difficult obstacles lie in the path of clarification but an active learning process allows us to try and progress.'

'Oh. I thought I had asked a simple question and you have pointed out so many complications.'

'Life itself is complicated. How can any question be simple?'

'What philosophy, professor!'

'It is the philosophy of life itself, if I may say so. But I am a simple man trying to answer complicated questions in a simple way in order to avoid complications in the minds of students.'

'I'm sure the director will be pleased to know that such efforts are being made to educate the students.'

'Ah, we all want to educate the students but things are never so simple.'

'Why?'

'Heavy committee responsibilities,' said Nilakantan with a heavy sigh. 'Heavy indeed. A great burden.'

'You are talking about the AICTE committee?'

'But of course. Director proposes and man disposes.'

'Woman also... I understand Professor Thilaka is also involved in the deliberations?'

Nilakantan frowned. Nallakannu was okay as far as these things went and good for the occasional bit of gossip and quasi-academic to-and-froing, but he was one of *them* and as such abundant caution was called for.

'Yes.'

Nallakannu waited for further enlightenment. None was forthcoming. 'I understand that...uhm, various non-academic matters also fall under the purview of the committee.'

'Indeed.'

'I was walking past Professor Thilaka's office and she was shouting loudly about the ladies' bathroom and the committee.'

This Nilakantan could believe. Like some female politicians belonging to *those* castes, Thilaka chose to express her opinions at full volume. The sound of her voice echoing through the corridors formed a large part of the nostalgic recollections of those who had passed out from the institute. For those condemned to occupy those same corridors as indentured residents that voice was a reminder of their continued servitude.

'What was she saying?'

Nallakannu leaned closer and lowered his voice. 'See, this is a delicate matter, which is why I came to see you. She said you were using the aforesaid ladies' bathroom and asking her to clean it as part of committee responsibilities. In fact,' his voice was now little more than a loud whisper, 'she was telling this to those students, the Social Justice Forum students.'

Rage, fear and loathing overcame Nilakantan. Rage at the outright lies and outlandish allegations. He had never asked that bloody woman to clean any bathroom, but the devious bitch had cleverly twisted his eminently sensible suggestions into caste-worthy allegations. What a loathsome, perverted woman! On top of everything, she had set those wild dogs from the Social Justice Forum primed with the scent of social injustice on his tracks. For a few minutes he was speechless and in the grip of raging fury. His voice eventually returned, shorn of eloquence.

'I...I...I...'

Nallakannu nodded sympathetically and encouragingly.

'I...I...I...'

Like an Ambassador spluttering to life, his thoughts finally found voice.

'I have never heard such false accusations. God is my witness that I have never used the ladies' toilet. So many years I have served the cause of education. When, in the cause of education, I have had the need to commit nuisance I have done so in the appropriate location only. Goddess Saraswati is my witness in this regard. My humble self has always been in the service of Goddess Saraswati herself, selflessly serving. You hear, Professor Nallakannu, selflessly serving…' His thoughts found an unexpected anchor. 'As I was explaining to you… to the students outside class even… I have been spending time clarifying difficult questions relating to contingent liabilities, questions that are subject matter for international committees… All this I have been doing out of service to these students from Meerut and Kurukshetra… students who are not even familiar with the sweet sounds of Tamil, students who know nothing about Thirukkural even. Perhaps saint Thiruvalluvar has opined on the true meaning of contingent liabilities as he has on so many important concepts.'

'Saint Thiruvalluvar,' echoed Nallakannu with suitable reverence.

'Do you know,' continued Nilakantan, 'that I had submitted a proposal for a course called Thirukkural on Management. The director said he would form a committee to study the proposal. I have been patiently awaiting the outcome of the deliberations of that committee for the last six months. And now here I am, accused without means of adequate defence, a finger outrageously pointed at me by that terrible lady who gives me a daily headache with all that shouting.'

His job done, Nallakannu gave a shrug and left.

Constituting a Committee

Well away from the tempests blowing through the institute, policy was being made amid the lush lawns and purposeful activity of Lutyens's Delhi.

A low buzz of conversation, cultured laughter, and an atmosphere as weighty as the luminaries who were strolling in filled the large conference room. Thick carpets made for a hushed ambience. A long table filled the room. Microphones at frequent intervals ensured that voices needn't be raised. Name tags were placed with careful consideration for the layered nuances of hierarchy. Thick folders stuffed with agenda papers were placed before each seat to remind everyone of the gravity of the day's proceedings. Uniformed bearers with plumed turbans served tea and coffee in expensive chinaware. Assistants scurried in and out on last-minute errands making sure the deliberations were not in any way interrupted.

Everyone knew their place in the pecking order; everyone other than the gentleman at the pinnacle of the order stole discreet glances at that worthy's teacup even as they exchanged gossip and information.

His habits were well known. He had developed the knack of finishing his cuppa fifteen seconds before the scheduled start of the meeting. The diktats of hierarchy meant that the pecking order had to be seated before its head. Waiting for someone to take their seat was not something heads took to kindly. They had, after all, waited more than thirty long years for the privilege of having everyone else wait for them.

The Secretary of the Ministry of Human Resources Development, Rajesh Ranjan, put down his cup, glanced quickly at his Rolex and took his seat at the centre of the table. The pecking order was clear: those at the end of the table were at the lowest level of the pecking order. For them, a seat at that table was itself a privilege.

'Ladies and gentlemen, a very good morning to you all,' the secretary started. A reciprocative murmur rippled around the table. 'You must be aware that in his address to panchayat representatives in Kohima last week, the prime minister stressed on the imperatives of modern management education. India seeks to take her place with developed countries and a modern managerial temper is an essential concomitant if that goal is to be achieved quickly.' Looking up from his prepared opening remarks, the secretary was pleased to see that notes were being taken. 'It is incumbent on this ministry,' he continued, 'to lay the groundwork for the development of a modern management outlook. We are here to fulfil the PM's vision by developing a detailed set of guidelines for management institutes to follow. We will constitute working groups to update existing AICTE and UGC norms keeping in mind twenty-first-century management paradigms. The PM has personally tasked me with incorporating cutting-edge concepts and practices into the guidelines and norms. We have been asked to consult with the giants of modern management in this endeavour of ours. We have been given a tight deadline: the final guidelines and norms need to be in place by the coming academic year. We need to have a concrete working plan at the conclusion of today's meeting and the working groups we shall be setting up today will be tasked with developing guidelines and norms in their respective areas, keeping this deadline in mind.

'Please note that I shall be preparing a detailed concept note for the committee of secretaries based on these recommendations. In turn they will prepare a white paper to be presented to the Group of Ministers, and based on that body's recommended policy actions, the PM might choose to constitute an empowered Group of Ministers to study implementation issues. Time, clearly, is of the essence and we might need to incorporate modern management practices to shepherd this process through. That would be entirely appropriate given the subject matter of our deliberations.'

He looked around once more, noting the alert looks and poised pens.

'That concludes my opening remarks, friends. Unfortunately, I will not be taking any further part in deliberations since I have to accompany my minister as part of our official delegation to the UNESCO conference on sanitation issues in pre-primary schools being held in Montevideo. My colleague, the additional secretary, will conduct the rest of the meeting on my behalf. I do have some unofficial remarks to make, however.' He bestowed a meaningful look at each of the attendees as he looked around the room. 'To reiterate, these are unofficial remarks.' The co-conspirators nodded their understanding and put their pens down.

'We all understand that all of this is essentially a waste of time. The IIMs will probably protest about undue interference from the ministry and, between you and me, will likely get away with it. Ditto the IITs, given their legal status which has been defined by an act of Parliament. The deemed universities are run by politicians and will make a loud noise about protecting their autonomy. Again, given the politics involved, they will get away with it. So our whipping boys are the second- and third-tier outfits. They probably cannot tell a paradigm from a concept and nothing we tell them is going to make the slightest difference to the crap they dish out in bucket-loads. So the real point of this exercise is to come up with a nice-looking report with some updated jargon and make some noise in the press before getting back to the really important stuff that is our daily bread and butter.'

The secretary paused meaningfully. Everyone was on high alert. 'One more thing. The PM has been taking yoga classes from this…ah…gentleman who fancies himself an expert. We need to co-opt him. Political exigencies. Any questions?'

A few hands went up, the bottom of the pyramid trying to impress the summit. A nod.

'Sir, a clarification. This yoga chappie. We are looking for his management expertise?'

'Something like that, yes.'

'Sir, unofficially, we are not looking at wholesale changes, are we?'

'Unofficially, what matters is the appearance of change rather than change itself. What matters is that we are seen to be doing something. Appearances are key in this, as they are in everything that we do. Unofficially, of course.'

'Sir, is this an appropriate place to promote the public–private partnership paradigm?'

'Four Ps, eh. I like that. Mind you, we seem to be drowning in paradigms. Pity when piles of people try to parrot a particular phrase. Forces us to mind our Ps and Qs.' Laughter. A pleased smile crossed the secretary's face. 'But yes, given the short attention spans that seem to be endemic these days, pithy acronyms and catchy phrases are good substitutes for matter and thought. So anything you can come up with, yes.'

The additional secretary coughed discreetly.

'Yes?'

'Expenses… We will need to survey some of the existing stuff…'

'Ah. Well, it could be argued that this falls under the National Literacy Mission, the subject matter being management literacy which, as the PM has pointed out, is a pressing national need. And since the finance minister has been very generous as far as the Literacy Mission is concerned, we needn't dip into ministry funds, if you get my drift. Have someone put together a budget and I'll have the minister sign off once Montevideo is off his mind.'

They had been asked to come at 10 a.m. and it was now close to 11.

An assistant had come out with a message some twenty minutes earlier: Swamiji was meditating but was aware of his morning appointments and would be with them in a little while.

The PM's yoga teacher had provoked an involved discussion about protocol at the ministry. The secretary had been unable to provide guidance given his preoccupations in Montevideo. The additional secretary had met his juniors several times to sort out the intricacies of the relevant protocol issues. Agreement was finally reached that the invite to the PM's personal yoga teacher had to come from someone more senior than an upper-division clerk. There was also general agreement that he was utterly undeserving of a secretary-level invite. That left the ministry's bureaucrats plenty to chew over. There was an understandable reluctance to volunteer for the task. Carrots, sticks, the protocol book all came into play and an extremely reluctant joint secretary accompanied by a deputy secretary (someone had to carry the joint secretary's briefcase) eventually made their way to the yoga teacher's establishment.

The establishment was clearly a commercial success. Large, well-maintained grounds with peacocks wandering the lawns, distant sounds of chanting, bhajans and discourses, an air of purposeful tranquillity, knots of kurta-clad foreigners in earnest conversation: all in all, an effective advertisement for Indian spirituality.

The secretaries waited in sullen silence.

Another assistant came by. Swamiji would be free shortly. Could they remove their footwear, socks included? And touching swamiji's feet was ashram protocol. He didn't insist on these things, of course, but respect needed to be given to someone of his attainments and so...

The secretaries' large stomachs and tight pants made this something of a stretch. Having to follow this up by sitting cross-legged on a mat kept them gasping for breath longer than they had anticipated. The prostrations done with, the yoga teacher added to their difficulties by staring fixedly at them and saying nothing.

The deputy secretary was the first to recover his breath and speech.

'Sir,' he began.

'People usually address me as Poojya Guruji.'

'Okay. Sorry. Poojya Guruji, I am Santosh Hota, deputy secretary in the HRD ministry and this is Shri Akshay Sinha, joint secretary.'

Poojya Guruji gave the slightest nod of acknowledgment.

'Our ministry has been tasked by the prime minister with revamping the management curriculum currently on offer in India keeping in mind the exigencies of our times. We will be working with management experts, practitioners and academicians to bring in cutting-edge ideas and pedagogical approaches to management education. The prime minister has told our secretary that you have given much thought to these matters. We would like to invite you as an expert on our panel of advisors. The ministry hopes to benefit from your insights into management education.' Sinha spoke with as much sincerity as he could muster. Plus, he was the senior man and one never knew how Poojya Gurujis would react to being invited by mere deputy secretaries.

Silence. After being stared at for a while, they began to wilt. Sweat beaded their brows and upper lips despite the climate-controlled environs.

'It has taken me many years, but the Lord has seen it fit to bless me with insights into the human condition. Some feel that these insights have great significance, but my claiming the same would betray a lack of modesty. Modesty is a virtue, of course, and the lack of it a vice. The universe is vast and its treasures uncountable. The insights I have been blessed with constitute but a small fraction of the treasure-house of knowledge that the benevolent Lord has created for our enrichment and enlightenment. To have an ego in the face of such overwhelming ignorance is wrong. Egos are for small minds and the ignorant. I subsumed my ego years ago at the lotus feet of the Lord. So when I say that it is not entirely appropriate for a joint secretary to deliver an invitation to me, it is not because I find it objectionable or because my ego doesn't permit it. I am an insignificant man and my ego irrelevant. In fact, as I just mentioned, my ego has ceased to exist. However, the rich body of knowledge and insight which I have been permitted to get a glimpse of thanks to the generosity of a benevolent deity demands respect. This respect is due not to me personally but to that knowledge of which I happen to be the bearer. I am just a vessel, but respect is due to what is contained in that vessel. Particularly since you hope to benefit from those deep, beautiful and powerful insights.'

'Poojya Guruji, I don't understand.'

'Respect for the knowledge of which I am a mere vessel would indicate a more appropriate mode of deliverance of the invitation.'

'Oh, you mean…'

'If I may inquire, why hasn't it been possible for the minister…?'

'Poojya Guruji, he is away in Uruguay attending a conference.'

'Your secretary?'

'I'm sorry, he is attending the same conference.'

'If I may be so rude as to enquire, what constitutes the subject matter of this conference?'

'Sir…oh…Poojya Guruji, it is the UNESCO conference on sanitation issues in pre-primary schools.'

'Ah, sanitation issues in pre-primary schools. An important topic, I am sure, which takes precedence over the contribution of Indian spiritual thought to modern management.'

'No, well, it is not exactly like that…'

'Then what exactly *is* it like?'

'The conference was scheduled much earlier. There was no thought…it was not our intention at all… You see we are on a very tight deadline for this… The PM desires…'

'Haste makes waste.'

'Yes, sir…sorry…Poojya Guruji.'

'You see, even the West has relevant things to tell us. I keep an open mind on these matters. Timing is all important. Take Karna. A most unfortunate man with a most unfortunate destiny. Why? Timing. An unseemly desire on the part of fate to hurry things along, to rush things to a conclusion. Gentlemen, I will be happy to meet your minister when he returns from his important deliberations in Montevideo. Do convey my regards to him.'

Human Resource Management I

'Professor Agarwal, how can I meet the director with these minutes?'

'Arre, Sambandham sahib, you have the full backing of the committee. The resolution is a unanimous one, no less, and we are all standing behind it 100 per cent.'

Which, Sambandham thought, was precisely the problem.

He hadn't slept for three nights. He had snapped at his wife and had been snapped back at in return. The to and fro had continued with unrelenting ferocity with his beloved daughter taking her mother's side.

If he told the director that he had not been party to the decision, he would have his colleagues stacked up against him with the minutes to back them up. And if he went along with the fiction that the recommendations were unanimous, an episode of extreme unpleasantness vis-à-vis the director was a near certainty. Taking sick leave was out of the question given the situation at home. Distraught, he had bungled his way through two classes, and even in his state could sense that those old standbys, the Kurukshetra–Panipat gang, were also turning against him.

Approaching Agarwal was an act of desperation. He knew that his fellow Tamilians were too caught up in their internecine quarrels to be of help. Like them, he loathed North Indians. But Agarwal was a shrewd fellow and the one most likely to come up with something constructive. Even so, he had never expected this from Agarwal: stonewalling with the blandest of expressions. Damned bania.

'Professor Agarwal, I know I have the full backing of the committee. You yourself have pointed this out. So why shouldn't the full committee meet the director and jointly explain the position? That way the director can see for himself how unanimous we are.'

'Sambandhamji, it is looking to me like you are afraid to see the director.'

'No, no, no, no. Not at all,' Sambandham spluttered.

'Furthermore, it is looking to me like there must be a good reason why the director has entrusted you with the chairmanship of this important committee. With chairmanship comes great responsibility which the director has entrusted in your good self. Who better than the chairman to explain the thinking behind the unanimous resolution? You yourself tell me.'

In his distress Sambandham took off his glasses and wiped them on his shirt. Putting them back on he looked at Agarwal through smudged fingerprints, aware that he looked like a caricature of an absent-minded professor. The unfairness of it all overwhelmed him. He was a helpless figure surrounded by malevolent forces intent on humiliating him. All those years of toil, the toe-hold by toe-hold scrabble up a slippery and treacherous career path, had led him to this, a humiliating end to his career. A deluge of emotions overwhelmed him. He burst into tears.

'Sambandhamji, Sambandhamji, why are you crying?' Dealing with an adult male in full emotional spate was not something Agarwal had had to do in his many years as an academic. Yes, there had been failures to pass examinations, failed love affairs, deaths, and the like, but those were ritual occasions with known scripts. Why was this man behaving like this? Was it something Agarwal had said? Was he supposed to console his colleague? These Madrasis were prone to extreme over-reactions and he was wary of what might happen if he patted Sambandham's shoulder or did something equally innocuous.

He fidgeted nervously, interjecting an occasional 'professorji, professorji', as he waited for this human train wreck to run its course and hopefully reach a salvageable destination. Which it eventually did, with an assortment of sniffles, suppressed sobs and a few involuntary snorts.

Embarrassed now, in addition to being emotionally overwhelmed, Sambandham got up to leave. News of his humiliation would be hitting the airwaves soon and the only thing left for him to do was to put in his papers, pack his bags and try to resurrect what he could of his career elsewhere.

'I'm sorry, Professor Agarwal,' Sambandham said in a muffled monotone, 'I have been wasting your time. Now I shall go.'

Agarwal jumped up. He couldn't let this man go out in this state. News that a card-carrying Tamilian had been seen exiting a North Indian's office in tears would only mean trouble for him. Visions of Thilaka and Anbuchezian at their loudest, and the likelihood that they would be joined by others with a sense of grievance and time to spare, led to Sambandham being manhandled back into his chair, given a handkerchief and a glass of water and cooed over with as much sympathy as Agarwal could muster.

The sniffling stopped and Sambandham blew his nose loudly into Agarwal's handkerchief. Agarwal swallowed hard and said nothing.

'Thank you, professor. Sorry once more. Very difficult situation I find myself in. Most difficult. Now I shall be going.'

'Arre, why are you going? Where might you be going? Sit here. I shall order tea, then we can discuss these matters.'

'I am not going to that bloody canteen.' Sambandham found his normal voice. 'They don't clean tables, they have no respect for senior faculty like me, and on top of everything AICTE discovers rats. I am asking you this: Is it any surprise that two rats are being discovered when tables are not being cleaned and respect is not being given? Green committee recommendations have been accepted *in toto* and we, our committee, has to find an AICTE-approved rat catcher. Tell me, Professor Agarwal, is this fair?'

'You are absolutely right, Sambandhamji. Absolutely unfair, situation is. Hundred per cent agreed. We shall discuss further steps. But cup of tea first, if I may.'

'I told you I am not going to that bloody canteen.'

'No need to go. I shall ask for tea here.'

'They bring tea to your room? You know, I asked that stupid canteen supervisor once for tea in my room and he said it was against employee union rules. He said there would be a dharna by canteen employees followed by work to rule and then an indefinite strike if faculty wanted tea in their room. You want tea, you go to canteen at specified times – those were his very words.'

'Sambandhamji, some little advice. These are all situations to be managed. We are in a management institute; we have to manage the situation, that is my motto. Practical management, I call it. You know that boy in the kitchen? I give him ten rupees a month and I get tea–coffee in my room. Practical solution. No rats, no dirty table, no problems. So, tea?'

Stunned by this casual run around the rules, Sambandham could only nod.

The tea was duly served and sipped, Sambandham noting in passing that it bore little resemblance to the stuff dished out in the rat-infested canteen.

'Sambandhamji, action must be taken.'

Fortified by good tea, and rid of excess emotions, Sambandham felt emboldened. 'Collective action only, Professor Agarwal. It is a collective problem.'

'United we stand, divided we fall.'

'Yes, that is my opinion also. What are your suggestions?'

'Immediate problem: rats in canteen. Two numbers as noted already, perhaps even more. Health problem.'

'Health is wealth, Professor Agarwal.'

'Indeed it is. And we are training our students in the making and management of wealth. Without health, what wealth is there to manage? So, first and foremost, a collective protest against canteen conditions is needed.'

'Yes.'

'The next issue is that our committee under your esteemed chairmanship has been given the task of getting rid of the aforementioned rats. Now, I ask you, were we responsible for the presence of the rats in the first place?'

'Of course not. That green committee...'

'Indeed. A problem not made by us. So we shall have a secondary protest wherein we shall discuss with our committee colleagues and request the director to direct those who created the problem to resolve it.'

They sipped tea. Agarwal was relieved at having been able to reach common ground with his colleague, relieved too that the emotional minefield had been traversed. Sambandham was relieved that he would not have to face the director alone.

Twenty-four (across): A bagged relative (6). The director sat hunched over the newspaper, chin on knuckles. He stared hard, trying to will the words into sense and obedience. No luck. He leaned back, attempting a different perspective on the puzzle. No luck there either. He refolded the newspaper, minding the creases, hiding away distracting snippets of news, and refocused his attention on the problem.

At an early age he had inadvertently topped his class, leading his parents to assume a latent genius which subsequent years (and exams) proved illusory. He (and his doting parents) had carried on under the assumption that his genius was real, and that the disappointments which followed were the result of unanticipated and unfair circumstances and forces.

Secure in his innate brilliance, he neglected those old-fashioned virtues of toil and perseverance when he took up a job as a business executive. A lack of progress in his management career was then put down to the same forces that had conspired to hide his academic worth. In time, he came to realize that what he really needed was a sinecure that demanded little of him and would provide him the time and wherewithal to pursue his hobbies and interests without interruption.

He became dimly aware of a commotion of sorts outside, of raised voices and insistent arguments. For a moment there, 24 (across) was within reach, but the disturbance blew away the thought that had been taking shape at the fringes of his consciousness and brought him back to annoying reality. He frowned. There always seemed to be someone or something to disturb the contemplative silence he had spent his life searching for. He hoped Jagan would do the needful.

Jagan was good at keeping intruders out, much better than that ineffectual Mrs Gopalan. As a result he was prepared to overlook Jagan's other deficiencies, which included an insatiable curiosity about files and papers that were not his concern and a brusqueness of manner which sometimes put callers off. That brusqueness was an ally when it came to pesky students and faculty. The uproar outside continued.

He thanked Jagan silently and was trying to recapture the fleeting thought about 24 (across) when the door burst open, depositing a clamorous group of faculty and an enraged Jagan into the sanctum sanctorum.

His laptop was shut, his newspaper lay open with the unfinished crossword. No time to gather thoughts, no time to set up the pretence of a working desktop, no time to be seen committing great thoughts to his computer's memory. He could only gape in shock as the vocal mob invaded his office and crowded around his desk.

'Sir, sorry, sir, too many peoples pushing, shouting...' Jagan.

'We are outraged. We are upset. We protest strongly.' Thilaka.

Emphatic hammering on the desk. Anbuchezian.

Having incited the protest, Agarwal discreetly held back, part of the body rather than the head of the protest. Further back, on the fringes, Sambandham tried his best to look inconsequential, to blend into the crowd, to do anything to avoid creating the impression that he was in any way responsible for this.

Polite words or standard expressions of welcome seemed inadequate and somehow inappropriate in the face of this appalling outrage. The director continued to gape and swallowed hard as he struggled to find words appropriate to the situation.

'Who do you think we are? Are we here to teach or to catch rats?'

'My ancestors were forced by you upper castes to catch rats and clean bathrooms.'

Each word was accompanied by a loud thump on the table. There was an essential physicality to Anbuchezian, most evident when he was upset, and he was well beyond mere anger by now.

'I'm sorry. I'm confused. But what is the matter? What has happened? Why are you so upset?'

'Look at him! He is asking us why we are upset! And while we have been working hard what has he been doing? A crossword puzzle!' Thilaka snatched up the newspaper and waved it around. 'See, that's why Jagatrakshagan has tried to prevent us from entering. So his master can do his crossword in peace. And while he is busy with his puzzle, what does he want us to do? Run after rats!'

'What's all this about rats? Will you please stop shouting? We can discuss this peaceably.'

'Deep insults you have given us and you want peace? For centuries we have suffered. Thousands of years we have suffered. That fool Manu, law-giver you call him, what sort of law he is giving? Bloody fool law!'

'If you would only tell me what this is about,

Professor Anbuchezian! You are an honoured and distinguished member of our faculty whose efforts have been deeply appreciated by the students and the management.'

'Then why am I not getting promotions? You tell me this. Because I am not upper caste?' More desk thumping followed.

'I assure you, Professor Anbuchezian, that caste plays no role in the evaluation of faculty.'

'What? What did you say? Did you all listen to him? Government rules are not being followed in promotions of faculty.'

'Professor, professor, please. That is not what I said. You misunderstood what I said.'

'You yourself are saying caste plays no role. Government is saying, Periyar is saying, I am saying, the law is also saying that reservation is a must. Our beloved Dr Anna is saying that reservation is must. Laws have been passed. And you are saying that caste plays no role. You are a dangerous man, but mind it. I too can complain to the government. In fact, I shall be complaining.'

'All promotions in this institute are as per government regulations. That's what I'm trying to say. Individual evaluations are completely fair. There is no discrimination on the basis of caste.'

'This man is being very clever. Playing with words and all. Tricking words and cleverness all the time. But not this time. Justice! Justice for all!'

'Professor! Please!'

Agarwal didn't like the way the discussion was going. Left to his devices Anbuchezian was capable of holding forth on caste injustice for hours. These rants were repetitive and generated a great deal of heat but little light. There was little to be gained by letting things run their course, so he sidled up to Thilaka and quietly tapped her shoulder.

'Rat, rat,' he whispered.

She got the message.

'Professor Anbuchezian has raised important issues that must be discussed in depth,' she shouted. 'We demand a full faculty meeting for a meaningful discussion and resolution of those issues. But first we would like to discuss the issue of the rats.'

'Two numbers of rats,' said a voice from the back.

'Madam and gentlemen,' said the director shaking his head, 'what rats? Could you please tell me what it is about the rats...'

'The rats in the canteen. Here, this is from your office.'

A much-handled sheet of paper, a copy of the original AICTE missive, was handed over.

Frowning, the director looked at it. 'This is a communication from AICTE about certain lacunae observed in the functioning of the institute. I had requested a committee headed by Professor Sambandham to suggest ways of resolving these issues. Is Professor Sambandham here? He can answer your questions.'

Sambandham shrank back and hid behind one of

his larger colleagues.

'Director sir, you are evading the issue. Look at observation number nine. Here it is.'

'Mmmm, okay. Professor Sambandham's committee was to suggest an AICTE-certified rat exterminator. Surely that would fall within the purview of the committee. After all, I'm not asking you to personally find and kill the rats.' The director had forgotten his initial fright and was getting annoyed. Why did these idiots have to make a mountain of every little molehill? They obviously had too little work to do and he needed to increase their teaching load – idle minds, devil's workshop, etc. etc.

'How did the rats get in the canteen in the first place?' asked Thilaka. 'Have you thought about that?'

The director looked wide-eyed at her. She must be even loonier than he had thought. 'What are you getting at? Am I supposed to know the provenance of every rat on this campus?'

'*You* are responsible for those rats!'

'Me? Professor Thilakavathi, of all the things I have heard in my tenure as director, this takes the cake. What else are you going to accuse me of now? And, anyway, why isn't Professor Sambandham here? This was his responsibility; he should be here to answer these questions.'

'You had appointed me, professors Agarwal, Anbuchezian and Nilakantan to the committee as well. Something you appear to have forgotten.'

'Yes, yes, I mean no, I haven't forgotten that you are

on the committee too, but as chairman, that would be Professor Sambandham's primary responsibility.'

'So you agree that you had asked the committee to look into the extermination of these rats?'

'Look, I say, what is...'

'Answer me directly. Did you or did you not?'

'Professor Thilakavathi, I will not be talked to in this fashion. I am busy and have no desire to carry on this ridiculous discussion.'

'Busy? What were you doing when we came in?' She turned to her restive colleagues. 'What was he busy doing?'

'Crossword!'

'And you have conveniently forgotten that you had constituted a committee on green campus which recommended cutting back on the cleaning of the canteen. Which was accepted by *you*. And as a direct consequence we have rats running around in the canteen. And, having created this rat menace in this campus, you ask us, the faculty, to find ways of exterminating the rats. We are teachers, not rat exterminators!'

Thilakavathi thumped the table to emphasize the point.

'Director down down, director down down,' the chant, started surreptitiously by some anonymous member of the throng, caught on and filled the room.

Upset, angry, scared, at his wits' end, the director could only stare helplessly. He wrung his hands and tried to remonstrate, to little effect. The crossword had been snatched up by someone: 24 (across) was destined to remain unsolved. Random, wild feelings peppered his thoughts. How on earth was he going to get out of this? How was this going to end? When was this going to end?

As if answering an unspoken summons, a group of uniformed security men barged in, swinging lathis and shouting at the faculty to leave. Unnoticed, Jagan had slipped out of the room and summoned help. There was a scramble to avoid the lathis and another for the door. Faculty solidarity gave way to self-preservation. Minor scuffles, much pushing and shoving and general unruliness marked the exit.

'Okay sir?' inquired the head of the security detail. Jagan was hovering around solicitously, trying to restore some order in the battered office.

Shaken, the director nodded his thanks. 'It was good that you came. Things were getting out of hand.' He was aware that there would be more to come, that this reprieve was temporary. Time, though, to savour the temporary peace and to think about some sick leave. After all, good managers and good generals sometimes called for a strategic vacation from the battlefield.

Executive Health

'Sir, the joint chancellor is calling and wishes to see you.'

Shit! He had called in sick, mentioning that his doctor had prescribed bed rest, preferably for a week at the least.

It had taken the director a day or two to recover from the invasion of his office but, eventually, with a book at hand, cricket on TV and the prospect of an uninterrupted day ahead, a feeling of mellow well-being had settled like a comfortable blanket around him. Until this. All of it felt like a conspiracy to deny him some well-deserved moments of peace.

'Jagan, didn't you tell him I was sick?'

'Yes, but he is still wanting to see you. In his office. Urgently.'

The director groaned.

'Did he say what this was about?'

'No, sir. Only that urgently he is wishing to see you.'

He drove out to the joint chancellor's office thinking dark thoughts and pondering alternative career paths.

Someone somewhere had to appreciate what he had to offer and provide him with what he needed. An interview with that crude, semi-literate womanizer was not what he needed. A long wait in the ante-room without tea or coffee for sustenance was not what he needed. The large photograph of the chancellor kept him company while he waited. His own thoughts were far gloomier and darker than those of the smiling chancellor. Eventually the summons came.

'Ah, Thiru director. Your health is suffering, I am told.'

'Yes, sir. A cold, mild fever, exhaustion. My doctor had prescribed rest.'

'Rest is good but service to the students is more important. The chancellor himself says that providing a good education is of foremost importance.'

The director nodded and waited.

'You see, Thiru director, I am receiving extremely disturbing news about your institute.'

'Disturbing news, sir? There must be some mistake somewhere.'

'Faculties creating disturbance in your office.'

Oh hell! How on earth had *he* got the news? Some spy, obviously, but who could the mole be? The place was probably riddled with informers. There were way too many suspects.

'Yes, sir, there was an unfortunate situation, but I am taking steps to bring things under control.'

'But you are not attending office due to your health suffering.'

'Yes, that's true. But I felt that it would be best to

let things cool off for a bit. Some of the faculty are excitable and I felt I shouldn't initiate action in the heat of the moment.'

'Why is the faculty creating disturbance like this?'

'It was a misunderstanding, sir, about the tasks allotted to some committees.'

'You are creating committees?'

'Yes, sir.'

'Of faculty?'

'Yes, sir.'

The joint chancellor shook his head disapprovingly. 'I don't like committees. Committees only create lots of trouble. Faculty committees create even more trouble. When faculty in one department creates trouble, faculty in other departments get all the wrong ideas. A small problem becomes a big problem. A big problem means story in the papers and TV and everything. A management person like you should know this. You shouldn't be teaching management if you don't. After all, what is management but making sure there is no problem. Not good, not good.'

'Sir, I feel that a participatory style of management...'

'See, these big words and all I don't know. All I know is that faculty of the Sundarambal Management Institute has created disturbance. In your office. In *your* office, Thiru director. You are the director, you should never allow such things. That is why you are director. If you cannot control your faculty, why are you the director? Tell me. I want a totally in-charge director, not this committee nonsense. Have you seen Parliament?

No? My uncle,' he pointed towards the chancellor's photograph, 'is an MP. Do you know why Parliament creates committees? For delay. If the government doesn't want a decision, it creates a committee. Committee means delay. If the opposition makes a noise, create a committee. Even a fool knows all this. And yet you create these committees. Foolish man! So kindly take charge. AICTE meeting must be successful. Remember, 125 more seats chancellor is wanting. Chancellor does not want delay, chancellor does not want noise, chancellor does not want committee, chancellor wants 125 more seats. And you, Thiru director, are going to get those seats. Understand?'

The director understood. He had no desire to go back to his office. He had his standing in the institute to think about. Jagan knew he was sick; he also knew of the joint chancellor's summons. If word got out that the director had gone from his sick bed to the joint chancellor's office and thence straight to his office, what little authority he had would erode even further. Whatever the consequences, he made his way back home. He was running a fever by the time he reached.

The faculty had taken a few days to regroup.

There was embarrassment at having turned tail post-haste when the security goons had showed up. A hushed, mortified silence filled the corridors.

The first whispers of defiance took their time surfacing. Furtive conversations and meetings began behind carefully closed doors. There was unease: did the director have informers? The joint chancellor? And Jagan, hadn't he called in the security? Why did they show up with such alacrity at the summons of a mere PA? And, most importantly, what to do next? They needed to find a common voice, they needed to meet. But where?

The fragile solidarity which had papered over disagreements and personal dislikes threatened to come apart on this crucial question. There was quick agreement that food was needed to fuel the discussion but the delicate concord began to give way when it came to the details. Preferences, restrictions, unspoken but evident caste-related constraints, fasting days, no-onions-on-Tuesdays kind of constraints – all were grounds for disputes, interpersonal conflagrations and ultimatums. After hours and days of simmering tension a consensus was reached.

And so, late one afternoon, classes and dictations done with, a subdued group gathered in a back room of Sastri's Meal Mess, a reputed establishment in town, with the proprietor S. Panchanathan Sastri himself in attendance. Idlis, vadais and degree coffee were served. Silent appreciation greeted the victuals and the discussions were put on hold until most of the coffee was drunk. There were some appreciative belches before they got down to the task at hand.

'That was excellent.' Nilakantan kicked off the discussion. 'I think we should thank Sastrigal for his service.'

Agreement all around, even Anbuchezian acquiescing with his old enemy.

'An army cannot march on an empty stomach!' exclaimed Thilaka, having added a kilo or two to an already substantial weight.

'Sorry, Madam Thilaka, but I do not understand this army connection. Pardon my ignorance.'

Thilaka took a deep breath before deciding not to disturb the general bonhomie. 'Professor Nallakannu, it is an old saying. You see, statistically, if you do not eat, you die. If you die, you cannot march.'

'Oh, yes yes yes. Now I understand the implications. You are suggesting a hunger strike.'

Loud protests.

'Hunger strikes and all are okay for Gandhiji,' said Sambandham. 'But not suitable for current conditions is my feeling.' The fate of his pot belly hung in the balance.

'What I mean,' persisted Nallakannu who felt that for once he had something substantive to contribute, 'is a chain hunger strike. Only one hour at a time and we can take turns. Very common these days and suitable for current conditions.'

'Hunger strike is an upper-caste activity,' shouted Anbuchezian, thumping the table. 'We lower-caste people are always hungry. We are cheated of food by the upper castes, so where is the need for hunger strike? We are always hungry. So I am suggesting what the great Periyar did: a protest feast. We will set up a pandal outside director's office and eat. Let that stupid man watch us eat. Then he will understand what is in our minds.'

'And in our stomachs,' concluded Agarwal, mystified as always by his colleagues' propensity to get sidetracked. 'Anbuchezianji, if I may ask, while yours is a most excellent and interesting suggestion...'

'Periyar himself has suggested this. I am only his humble servant.'

'Yes, of course. Periyarji was a great man,' continued Agarwal.

'And so was Thiruvalluvar.' Nilakantan was not about to let matters continue without adding a Brahmin to the mix. 'Thiruvalluvar also advocated good eating. Good for health was his prognosis. In fact, I have been advocating adding a class on Thiruvalluvar's ideas for management. But the director has again referred this to a committee...'

'Which committee?' Anbuchezian wanted to know. 'I would like to suggest inclusion of Periyar's management thoughts. Kindly inform me who the chairman of that committee is so I can make submission accordingly.'

'I do not know the composition of the aforementioned committee.'

'Does anyone know?'

Blank looks all around.

'How can the director constitute a committee on academic matters without consulting the faculty? That is the question I am asking,' Anbuchezian persisted.

'That man is fooling all of us. First he asks the faculty committee to kill rats. Second he constitutes a committee on important academic matters without consulting the faculty.'

'Also he is not including Periyar's management thought in the purview of said committee.'

'Madam, gentlemen, please, please. We are losing our focus. Let us remember why we are here.' Agarwal was once more on his feet attempting to get his wandering colleagues back in line. 'We are here, first and foremost, to consider how to protest the director's attack on faculty. Then we can protest his not listening to the genuine academic proposals put forward by the faculty. My good colleague Anbuchezianji has kindly suggested a novel form of protest as originally propounded by the great Periyarji.'

'Thiruvalluvar also suggested.'

'Yes, yes, Thiruvalluvarji has also propounded. An excellent suggestion also. But if I may ask, first, who will be paying for this protest-feast? Second, there is the matter of seeking agreement on a suitable menu. Third, pandal, service, etc. needs to be arranged. Fourth, if our stomachs are full, how can we effectively voice our protest? Myself, after a good meal, I want a good sleep. Snoring in my humble opinion reduces the effectiveness of protest.'

'Professor Agarwal, you are making many valid points. Four numbers of points, no less, as you yourself are pointing out. But what exactly are you suggesting?'

'Yes, Professor Agarwal. You must be having rich experiences from faculty protests in North India and whatnot.'

'Indeed yes. In fact, as you may know, my dissertation was on "Strike as a Means of Protest with Implications for Management". My field work was undertaken in the hosiery industry in Ludhiana. But I have participated in faculty actions as well, in Meerut and Kurukshetra. My observation is that there are essential differences in the South Indian scenario.'

'How so?'

'If I may put it this way, politics is aligned with labour in North. Here politics is aligned with management. Therein lies the problem.'

'What is the problem?'

'You see our chancellor?'

'Only his photograph.'

'No, no, you don't understand my point. Suppose you go to the police and say that director's security is beating you up. Now suppose joint chancellor gives simultaneous complaint to the police that you are beating up director's security. What will the police do?'

The thought of what the police would do in the circumstance outlined by Professor Agarwal reduced them to a very thoughtful silence. The thoughtful S. Panchanathan Sastri served them another round of coffee accompanied by excellent potato bondas. The food relieved some of the doom without dispelling it entirely.

Professor Nallakannu finally broke the silence. 'My brother is division IV clerk in Canara Bank. Once they protested by wearing banians to work. All customers were served wearing banians only.'

'You mean they were wearing only banians?' Professor Sambandham looked shocked.

'Only banians, yes.'

'What about pants, underwear and all?'

'Professor Sambandham, I am saying that they were not wearing only banians but also pant, underwear and all. But no shirt.'

'They went to work wearing only banians?'

'No, no, they took shirts off after reaching office. Thereafter banians only.'

'There is no way I am going to teach wearing a banian,' shouted Thilaka. 'You men will do anything to get a lady to undress. Damn sexists! Male chauvinist pigs!'

'Professor Thilaka, you are misunderstanding me. When did I say that you should wear a banian? I never want to see you wearing one.'

'I thought a lot of men would want to see me wearing a banian. Are you suggesting that I won't look good in one?'

The thought of Thilaka in a banian was more than Nallakannu could countenance. 'Yes, I mean no, but what I really mean... No, yes, no but surely you don't mean... I mean... No, but that is not what you should take to mean yes... I mean no...'

'Stop blabbering, Professor Nallakannu. You have a dirty mind.'

'Dirty is a state of mind, but mind you, dirty minds may be found in clean bodies and clean minds in dirty bodies, but that doesn't mean...'

'Stop blabbering, Professor Nilakantan. All you men have dirty minds. I'm sure you also have one.'

'My colleagues, enough, enough. Why do you fight

like this? In the North, faculty solidarity is extremely solid. Like the Fevicol ad, once stuck never parted. Solid against administration, solid for rights, solidarity against students as well. A solid wall.'

'Like the Red Fort?'

'Or Rahul Dravid?'

'Indeed, yes.'

'Solid red wall, then. But in the south, only Kerala has solid red walls. But even there you have CPM red, CPI red, etc. There is much confusion about the shade of red in the walls.'

'Red, white, blue – I don't care.'

'The French tricolour! Liberty, equality, fraternity! What stirring words! How could you say that those colours do not matter?' Thilaka was better read than the rest (the director excepted) and was always keen to display her erudition to her colleagues. Quite often, though, her efforts were lost on them. They stared at her, anticipating some elaboration. She sighed. The romance of the French Revolution, those stirring speeches at the barricades, those soaring ideals – and this reality.

'Gentlemen, we have been here two hours and still haven't decided how to protest. I need to go home soon. So what do we do?'

They looked around at each other.

'As Thiru Agarwal has pointed out, the chancellor is a powerful man.'

'We need to register a protest, but in a non-violent fashion so that the police does not get involved.'

'Somehow impact needs to be there. A protest with no impact is like a politician without money. Totally useless.'

'This banian idea…'

'I've already told you that this is a sexist, obscene suggestion made with the sole view of…'

'Madam, madam, kindly listen. I am suggesting that only men faculty wear banians.'

'Did Canara Bank management actually do anything when your brother and his colleagues wore banians?'

'My brother did not elaborate on that aspect.'

'So you will end up looking like complete fools without achieving anything. It is difficult enough to keep these bloody students under our thumb without ridiculing ourselves by showing up in the classrooms in banians.'

'Madam, what I am thinking is when AICTE surprise committee visits. We make our representation to management that if our demands are not met by then, we will protest on day of the AICTE visit by wearing banians. Men faculty only, madam.'

'Good suggestion I think. But chancellor and joint chancellor will not be happy.'

'I've got an idea.'

Everyone looked at Agarwal. Whatever they thought about North Indians in general, they had a healthy respect for his worldly wisdom and practical experience in dealing with recalcitrant managements.

'You see, we must ask, do we have a problem with joint chancellor and chancellor?'

Clearly not.

'And our worry, is it about the director or them?'

The director obviously did not merit a mention in this context.

'So, practical management is providing a solution. We are management faculty and therefore we need a management solution to our problem.'

True as far as it went, but where specifically were his thoughts taking him?

'Our charter of demands, we will take a three-pronged approach.'

'Trishul!'

'Exactly! Like Lord Shiva we shall make a three-pronged approach.'

Thilaka thought there was something obscene in all this talk about three-pronged approaches but held back. The female faculty had already been excused from participation in the three-pronged approach now that the banian issue had been resolved.

'In our representation, we will first demand that chancellor be given an honorary degree for his contributions to management. Our second demand is that the rat and toilet business be under the purview of committee on green campus since these problems were created by them in the first instance. Our third demand is a full and complete apology from the director for his physical assault on the assembled faculty. We will express our faith in the joint chancellor's leadership and if our just and fair demands are not met in toto we will stage our banian protest in front of the AICTE representatives. Three demands, trishul, and we shall be seeking the blessings of Lord Shiva for our just cause.'

There was excited agreement and a loud, happy babble of conversation.

'There is one more thing we can be adding to these just demands,' said Sambandham as the conversational bubble died down. 'That Jagan, he is always keeping the door shut, stopping faculty from meeting the director. Now he is also responsible for instigation of faculty assaults and all. I am demanding that he be dismissed herewith and Gopalan madam reinstated forthwith.'

'Also we can be demanding outcome of committee deliberations on Thiruvalluvar.'

'And inclusion of Periyar thoughts also.'

'These are just demands, I am not denying that. They are very vital demands, I agree. But too many demands are making our trishul into a fork. Too many prongs and the essence of protest gets diluted. You know that famous management saying, KISS: Keep it Simple but not Stupid. Have you ever seen Lord Shiva with a fork? No, because of a simple reason which Lord Shiva knew well before modern management practices, which are basically old Indian sayings for the benefit of Western audience. Trishul equals three-pronged approach which is better than five- or six-pronged approach which equals knife and fork, good only for eating omelette and other things. Not suited for Indian conditions. So, Sambandhamji, Nilakantanji and Anbuchezianji, your demands we shall take up also, but in due course.'

'Core competence we shall be sticking to, in other words.'

'Indeed.'

The Indian Management Tradition

'Management in the 21st century needs to shake off the shackles of outmoded ideas and practices rooted in industrial conglomerates of the 20th century. Today's interconnected and globalized society calls for an altogether different paradigm. The Global Village, Core Competency, the Bottom of the Pyramid – each of these is an idea forged in the crucible of practice in a world where the internet, global supply chains and rapid technological obsolescence combine to bring together global scales of operation with a focus on local needs, local mores and localized actions.'

The McKinsey partner, Akshay Joshi, paused to sip his Evian. He was one of a number of distinguished invitees called on to advice the committee constituted by the HRD ministry to give concrete shape to the PM's vision of a modern, managerial India. Joshi was there with industrialists, financiers and global management thinkers to voice their ideas on how to wrestle that unwieldy, bloated mess that was Indian management education into a lean, purposeful tool of transformation. Like the others in the room, he was expected to serve pro bono and spend days on end in confabulations. And, like the others, he knew that turning down the ministry's invite was not an option. 'Expert committees' were the government's chosen tool of transformation, and he knew that invitations to expert committees meant opportunities to rub shoulders with otherwise inaccessible bureaucrats and politicians in relatively stress-free, informal settings.

That was the idea at any rate. What he and his fellow distinguished invitees had failed to reckon with was the presence of Poojya Guruji in their midst.

Which is why, instead of the usual conference room with a long table, the 'experts' found themselves in a large unfurnished room with thin mattresses strewn about the floor. There were a handful of bolsters at one end, and doubts as to who would have the bolsters to lean on were quickly dispelled as a saffron-clad, bearded, middle-aged man was ushered in with more than the usual coterie of attendants in tow. He settled himself amongst the bolsters in the manner of a monarch making himself comfortable on his throne.

What followed was worse. While a clearing of the throat or a cracking of knuckles was adequate preamble for most, Poojya Guruji insisted on pranayamas, sitalis, surya namaskaras and sudarshana kriyas. Formal businesswear came in the way of these being completed to Guruji's satisfaction and they were subjected to a lecture on the benefits of yoga in these times of stress. Cups of grass juice followed before the proceedings got under way.

Thankfully, the ministry had had its way on a few things. Evian was on offer, the room was air-conditioned and the formal proceedings were initiated by the Secretary. An agenda including the order of speakers had been set and, to general relief, Poojya Guruji was not on the list of speakers. Why he was there, though, remained a mystery.

Given their global prominence and acknowledged managerial expertise, McKinsey and Company, represented by the Harvard-educated Akshay Joshi, led the day's proceedings.

Joshi had put down his glass and was poised to resume when Poojya Guruji intervened.

'Mr Joshi!'

Startled, Joshi looked up. 'Yes, sir?'

'Poojya Guruji.'

'I beg your pardon?'

'I am not one to attach any sort of value to titles. Titles, after all, have no relation to a person's true character. What connection the Duke of Edinburgh has with the city of Edinburgh has always been a mystery to me. Likewise the Duchess of York with York. And diplomats, routinely referred to as Their Excellencies, more often than not fail to excel at anything. That said, my followers have chosen to refer to me as their Poojya Guruji and who am I to go against their wishes? After all, the best managers take their subordinates' opinions on board and we are here to discuss management, aren't we?'

'I'm so sorry. But, Poojya Guruji, you had interrupted me...'

'Young man, I don't interrupt,' said Poojya Guruji. 'Interrupting life's cadences is a western habit. I was merely asking you to pause to contemplate some of life's verities. Take your company. How old is it?'

Joshi had no idea. He hazarded a guess. 'About eighty years old, sir.'

'Eighty years. A lifetime to most of us. My guru lived to a hundred and forty before being buried in an avalanche while meditating. But for most of us eighty is a lifetime, hopefully a fulfilling one. Do you know when the Gita was composed?'

'No Poojya Guruji.'

'Anyone else?'

Shakes of the head.

'Five thousand years ago. What is eighty years of McKinsey wisdom in the face of the mighty Gita?'

Silence. There was a general sagging of shoulders as the import of Poojya Guruji's words and presence became clearer.

'Being a prime minister means acquiring multitasking abilities and dealing with levels of stress that most of you can only guess at. One of the many things I am involved in is helping our PM deal with stress and in setting priorities. Important managerial skills as you would know. Do you know why the PM chose me to be part of this initiative?'

They did, but chose to closely guard their thoughts and feelings. Sullen silence reigned. Poojya Guruji looked around the room and caught no one's eye.

'I'll tell you. It's because I have been able to distil the essence of management from five thousand years of Indian wisdom. The Gita, the *Arthashastra*, the Upanishads and Patanjali's Yoga Nidras all contain pearls of managerial erudition whose surface Western thinkers and practitioners have barely scratched. You create a pearl by adding a grain of dirt to an oyster. Western thought has not progressed beyond that grain of dirt. We, on the other hand, have in our hands a beautiful pearl. What managerial education needs is a holistic study of that pearl. Mr Joshi, you talked about throwing off the shackles of outmoded ideas and about modern paradigms. But have you thought about the environment in which learning takes place?'

Joshi was thinking about what a bloody waste the morning was turning out to be. There was no way he could check his Blackberry without being seen. Worse, he hated it when someone interrupted him. And with this guruji character involved, and involved deeply by the look of things, prospects for business as a result of this pro bono participation looked extremely dim. Had he known this was how things were to be, he would have sent along some fresh-faced junior to mark attendance on McKinsey's behalf.

Joshi was not the only one to not have given thought to the 'environment in which learning took place'. An uneasy silence hung over the group.

'No? That's unfortunate, but is typical of Western inattention to detail. But let me enlighten you. The colour of the paint used in classrooms is crucial. I'm sure that none of you realized this. You see, when we yogis go out in search of enlightenment, we go to the Himalayas. Adi Sankara walked all the way from Kerala to the Himalayas. Why the mountains? Because of the colours. White glaciers all around, blue skies above. So without first painting classrooms white with blue ceilings, we will go nowhere. It is my humble suggestion that this be the first recommendation of this committee.'

Excerpts from the minutes of the meeting of the High-Powered Committee on Management Education in India:

After a fruitful discussion covering all aspects of management education in India including past and current practices, the following suggestions were made:

1. The Indian ethos in management should take primacy over passing Western fads. The current culture of structuring courses and materials around fashionable buzzwords needs to be revisited in light of this suggestion.
2. The role of the environment in which management education takes place has not received adequate attention. In particular, the committee recommends that management classes take place in rooms with blue ceilings and white walls. In order to minimize distractions and maximize the impact of this colour scheme, windows and doors should be painted white and kept shut during classes. White tube lights affixed to the walls are also recommended. Ceiling fans, if any, should be painted blue. Colour matching cards should be provided by the AICTE to ensure uniformity.

A sub-committee under the chairmanship of Poojya Guruji Sri Sri Sri Rambhakta Swami will ensure that the correct shade of blue is chosen.

3. In keeping with the ancient Guru–Shishya tradition where students learnt at the feet of their masters and keeping in mind the historical verity that knowledge and wisdom prospered when these traditions were followed, classrooms should be reconfigured to provide a platform for the guru and seating on the ground for students. The guru's platform should be made of naturally occurring materials such as mud, stone or wood. Cement, plastic and other similar materials should not be used. Likewise, the floor on which students sit must be of naturally occurring materials. A sub-committee under the chairmanship of Poojya Guruji Sri Sri Sri Rambhakta Swami will come up with a list of approved materials for both the gurus' platforms and the students' floors.
4. The ancient Latin saying '*sit mens sana in corpore sano*', which was copied from even more ancient Sanskrit texts, implies that the study of management is best undertaken by healthy students. A sub-committee under the chairmanship of Poojya Guruji Sri Sri Sri Rambhakta Swami will draw up a programme of yoga specifically designed for management students. Poojya Guruji Sri Sri Sri Rambhakta Swami assured the committee that his foundation would set up a yoga learning centre at every AICTE-approved management institute and at all IITs, central universities and IIMs. The committee placed on record its deep

appreciation to Poojya Guruji Sri Sri Sri Rambhakta Swami for his contribution.

5. Poojya Guruji Sri Sri Sri Rambhakta Swami pointed out that the benefits of the yoga programme would be enhanced when accompanied by changes in the students' dietary intake. A sub-committee under the chairmanship of Poojya Guruji Sri Sri Sri Rambhakta Swami will come up with a list of model menus for management students. AICTE shall make all efforts to ensure that management institutes implement the dietary recommendations of the sub-committee.
6. A discussion on funding the yoga learning centres followed. Both the HRD ministry and Poojya Guruji Sri Sri Sri Rambhakta Swami expressed their inability to fund this important activity. Representatives of industry felt that in light of the difficult conditions following the global financial crisis, they would not be in a position to contribute to the funding of this important activity. The committee therefore recommended that the yoga learning centres be funded by a special levy on all management students.
7. The committee had a detailed discussion of ancient texts and their relevance to modern management. The committee recommends that a course incorporating management learnings from ancient Indian texts be made a compulsory part of every AICTE-approved management course. The course would include both original material from, and commentaries on, the Bhagavad Gita, the Rig Veda, the Upanishads and

Kautilya's *Arthashastra*. A sub-committee under the chairmanship of Poojya Guruji Sri Sri Sri Rambhakta Swami will create a detailed syllabus for this course.

8. The committee directed the ministry to set up a secretariat to oversee the preparation of the final report incorporating suggestions made during the committee's deliberations and requested that a suitable budget be allocated to the same. The committee agreed to set up a cell in Poojya Guruji Sri Sri Sri Rambhakta Swami's ashram to coordinate the work of the sub-committees. A budget for the same would be decided in coordination with the PMO.
9. Representatives of McKinsey and Co., Tata Sons, Wipro, Infosys, L&T, Reliance Industries, ADAG and ICICI Bank regretted their inability to attend future meetings of the committee, citing pressing business commitments and the global financial crisis. The committee thanked them for their valuable contributions to the deliberations.

Being the secretary of a central ministry had its perks. People came to you, they listened to you and they did what you asked them to do. This Poojya Guruji character, though, had turned things on their head, to a point where the Secretary felt like a schoolboy taking dictation.

'But, Poojya Guruji…'

'Mr Ranjan, patience is a great virtue. Letting others

finish what they have to say is an equally important virtue. And having an open mind is perhaps the greatest of virtues. There is something truly beautiful about open minds.'

In addition to leaking hot air, thought the Secretary sourly.

'As I was saying, I feel that in order to provide a suitable context to the specific recommendations we have already agreed on, members of the committee should visit several business schools to observe first-hand current practices extant in business education. My ashram has planned retreats in several cities in South India. Perhaps it makes sense for me to visit some local business schools to see for myself what goes on in the guise of education.'

'Yes, Poojya Guruji.' Anything to bring this ruddy meeting to a close.

'But, and I feel this is crucial, these visits should not receive any prior publicity or notice. We need to see things as they are, not how others want us to see them.'

'But there is this court ruling about surprise inspections of educational establishments.'

'I beg your pardon?'

'There was a High Court judgment last year which stated that educational institutions should be given a minimum of 30 days' notice for any surprise inspection. The court is liable to take a serious view of any violation and affected institutions are very likely to approach the court for punitive relief.'

'That is ridiculous. Even the Upanishads say that

list of all AICTE-approved management institutes in the four southern states.'

'Certainly.'

'I would like the data in an Excel file defined by city, state and pin code.'

'That would take time. Collating all the data...'

'Am I to understand that the data is not readily available?'

'That was not the intent of my communication nor is it fair to impute that particular shade of meaning to a general statement containing the temporal possibilities inherent in fulfilling particular requirements whose dimensions leave open the likelihood of further calls on the scarce resources of the ministry.'

'I see. When Arjuna stood on the battlefield, uncertain about what he needed to do, Krishna stepped in to provide clarity about the role Arjuna was expected to play in the war. I shall endeavour to play Krishna to your Arjuna. I expect the information I requested, in the form I requested, by Friday. Should that not happen, I shall be constrained to hold a press conference in my capacity as a member of the committee to bemoan the ministry's inability to provide basic information to members of committees constituted at the suggestion of the PM. Furthermore, in view of the difficulties inherent in participating in the committee's deliberations without fully knowing the subject matter under consideration, I shall have no alternative but to regretfully tender my resignation to the PM. Good day, Mr Ranjan. I have several pressing matters to attend to.'

'I find his cavalier treatment of bureaucrats to be deeply disturbing. He is high-handed, arrogant and thoroughly offensive. Our colleagues over in the finance ministry might find his activities to be of considerable interest.'

Ranjan, Sinha and Hota were discussing Poojya Guruji and his unreasonable ways.

Ranjan, antennae honed from years of hearing viewpoints aired before a carefully considered consensus was reached, sensed the mood of his junior colleagues. He had planned this meeting as a routine let-off-some-steam exercise with no clear objective in mind. Many years in the IAS had inured him to some of the less pleasant aspects of political oversight over his activities and he had developed a sense of perspective over these intrusions into the even tenor of his existence. There was nothing that a peg or two at the nineteenth hole couldn't cure. These youngsters, though, allowed their equanimity to be easily disturbed. They would learn in due course that Poojya Guruji and his ilk needed to be listened to and humoured. They would also learn that there were ways of keeping unreasonable demands at bay indefinitely. While they would learn all this given enough time, he needed to find a more suitable outlet for their youthful energy and outrage.

'I'll handle all matters concerning our favourite yoga guru. I'll talk to the PMO and find a way to take care of this proposed trip of his. Meanwhile, we need to demonstrate to the entities we regulate that we mean business. Tell AICTE we will be accompanying them on their inspection tours. Form teams of two, attach yourselves to the AICTE teams and enjoy yourselves.'

'The PM-mandated study…'

'Is now in the hands of our Poojya Guruji. Once you boys and girls are off, I can truthfully tell him that we cannot man his secretariat. Between you and me, far better that the PMO follows up the PM's many initiatives. We have plenty on our plate as it is.'

Information Flow in Organizations II

'Yes?'

The joint chancellor's tone was not very welcoming and he had about him an air of wanting to get this over with as quickly as possible.

Not that the faculty hadn't tried to ingratiate themselves. They had been made to wait for over three hours before being granted an audience. Not knowing when that audience would materialize and knowing well that the busy-looking PA was likely keeping tabs on their behaviour, they spent their time gazing reverentially at the chancellor's photograph to a point where familiarity with that worthy's nasal hair, the mole on his right cheek and the neatly combed fans of hair emanating from his ear was complete. Three hours of reverential gazing meant serious strain on the facial nerves and muscles. This meant that when they prostrated themselves before the chancellor's photograph in the joint chancellor's office, there was a certain stiffness and a lack of the sort of noisy enthusiasm that Tamil politicians and businessmen take for granted from their acolytes.

'Sir, we are here to make a humble representation to your distinguished self,' Professor Agarwal began hesitantly.

'Speak to your director about it.'

'Sir, we tried to make a representation to the director but...'

'I have had very disturbing news of the disturbance created in the director's office. Are you people responsible for this disturbance?'

They had known this issue would likely be on the joint chancellor's agenda and there had been much discussion about how to deal with it. They didn't know how much had filtered back to the joint chancellor and were wary of potential informational bombshells. There had also been involved and impassioned negotiations about the team which would make the humble representation before him. Thilaka had been ruled out as she had been at the forefront of the fracas in the director's office. In addition, her weighty persona notwithstanding, the joint chancellor's proclivities with ladies needed to be considered. Anbuchezian had punctuated the proceedings in the director's office emphatically, too emphatically perhaps, to represent matters. Then there was the natural reluctance of the rest of the faculty to indulge in a tête-à-tête with the joint chancellor.

All of which meant that the chosen ones – Sambandham, Nilakantan and Agarwal – were most reluctant carriers of the torch.

'Not really, sir. We would definitely have preferred to go through proper channels but there was a marked reluctance on the director's part to entertain our humble requests. After all, sir, we are here only to serve yours and the chancellor's interests and the students' as well. We are assuring you of our fullest cooperation in all matters and only have a few humble matters for your consideration.'

'What is it?'

'Sir, we the management faculty all feel that chancellor's contribution to management should be recognized. He is a great management thinker.'

'Chancellor doesn't think. He is not like you faculty people. He is a man of action. He is a man of achievements. From humble beginnings our chancellor has achieved his way through action. Look at him!'

Once more, they looked at him.

'This is just exactly what we would like to recognize, sir. Our humble suggestion is to offer an honorary doctorate to our chancellor. He deserves so much more, perhaps he can be PM or president of United Nations even, but from our humble selves we are suggesting this small offering. A small token of our great regard and respect.'

'Hmm. Interesting proposal. What did your director say?'

'Sir, we were trying to make a representation to the director, being the official channel, but before we could finish stating our proposal, security forces curtailed the meeting. We were forcibly evicted.'

'Hmm. I shall bring up this matter for the chancellor's consideration; but he is a busy man. He has many occupations and preoccupations. Many matters are placed for his consideration. The chancellor's decision on all matters is final. You understand this?'

'Yes, sir. Of course, sir. We only wish for the chancellor's esteemed consideration of the matter. And, begging your pardon, just one more matter, if we may crave your indulgence, sir.'

'Yes?'

'Director is asking us to kill rats on the campus, sir.'

'What?'

'Sir, you see, the committee on green campus...'

'Committees? I have already warned the director about committees. The chancellor is always saying that committees mean delays. Next you will be saying that for killing rats also there is a committee.'

'Indeed, sir. The director has constituted a committee to look into killing rats.'

'Idiot! Fool! Buffalo! Dog! I have told him many times that I don't like this committee nonsense. If the chancellor hears about this he will shut the institute down and ask director to kill the bloody rats himself!'

'Yes, sir. Perhaps the chancellor's management techniques can be the subject of a new course which we can design in consultation with him. With your kind blessings and permission, of course.'

'Ah, another interesting proposal. Maybe you management faculty have interesting ideas after all. Certainly better than killing rats using committees, I think. Very interesting. I think even the chancellor will find it interesting.'

They all looked up at the photograph once more. They noticed a paan stain or two around the edges of the lips. Brylcreem and paan were clearly conducive to chancelloric thoughts. The joint chancellor cleared his throat noisily.

'Okay. I shall bring all these matters to the chancellor's attention. And the director, he can use rat poison instead of a faculty committee to kill the rats.'

'Professor Sambandham, can you give me a ride back home? My scooter has gone for service.'

Thilaka was resplendent in a pink sari adorned with serious quantities of bright embroidery work. The afternoon sun and the white-washed walls were mere props in the periphery of her universe. Sambandham tried hard to come up with an excuse. The problem with Thilaka was that she would never take no for an answer and was relentless in her use of logic to wear down any opposition. Sambandham, slow to think and even slower to give voice to his thoughts, knew he stood no chance. Even so…

'My wife…' he stuttered.

'I'm not stealing you, professor. Your wife has nothing to worry about. Unless, of course, you prefer that I take the bus.'

'No, no. I am not suggesting that. Not that, but… okay, okay. Yes, I mean.'

He imagined a thousand staring eyes as they left, and a thousand more as she wrapped a bangled arm around him to keep her balance. Self-conscious, acutely aware of that arm around his midriff, aware of her bulk wedged against his back, he tried to keep his balance.

As always, he didn't have his helmet on, one small point among many that marked the frontier in his marital conflicts, and for once he wished he had given in to his wife. With that embroidered pink sari and her jewellery glinting in the sun, he knew that Thilaka was attracting attention everywhere they went. He knew that curious eyes would follow that arm, work their way past his belly, and finally come to rest with shocked recognition on his face. Sober, sensitive Sambandham: seducer.

She shouted directions in his ear, which he followed like an automaton. The streets were familiar and despite his distracted thoughts he soon became aware that she lived in the general vicinity of his home. Worse luck.

She finally had him stop at a block of flats. He sat still, gunning his scooter and waiting for her to get off so he could ride off into oblivion. The bangled arm stayed put.

'Professor, aren't you coming in for a cup of coffee?'

'What? Sorry. No. Already late, wife waiting. Kindly excuse.'

'Five minutes only, professor. Are you feeling shy? I'm married too, so I won't eat you up. Don't worry, my coffee is excellent.' She laughed like a Wodehousian aunt and her mocking laughter seemed to echo back to him from the buildings all around.

Reluctantly, he got off. Reluctantly, he pushed his scooter into her building compound. Reluctantly, head hung low, he followed her up the stairs.

She busied herself in the kitchen while he stared at his feet, willing the minutes to hurry up.

'Haven't seen the director lately, have you?' she shouted cheerily.

'No,' he mumbled.

'Any news on that AICTE committee?'

Post the meeting with the joint chancellor, there had been the obligatory few hours in the mental decompression chamber: none of the three had been willing to brave the questions of their waiting colleagues and had quietly slipped home and switched off their mobiles. There had then been some discussion. They agreed on silence. The joint chancellor was known for his erratic ways. Far better that any news, any decisions, be put out by his office. In the meanwhile, the three agreed that they would say nothing and do nothing. The AICTE committee could atrophy, the rats could multiply, the lacunae could rest undisturbed. If the director did show up and summon them, they would proclaim their fealty to the joint chancellor and refer the director to him. Their faculty colleagues could stew in suspense.

'The matter is in the hands of the joint chancellor.'

'Here's your coffee. Sugar? Here. What did you tell him?'

'He was apprised of the facts.'

'And?'

'We did what we were told to do. As I said, we apprised him of the facts.'

'How did he react? Was he angry?'

Nosy bitch, he thought to himself.

'Madam, I was looking at my notes and failed to observe his reactions.'

'Surely you must have heard his tone of voice. Have your coffee. It will get cold otherwise.'

'He expressed his displeasure at what happened in the director's office. Otherwise he just listened and said nothing.'

'He must have said something.'

'We have left the matter in his hands.'

'So…are you planning to convene another meeting of the AICTE committee? What do you plan to do if the director asks for an update?'

'We will wait for the joint chancellor's decision.'

'Professor, you are trying your best to avoid answering my questions, aren't you?'

'No madam, but…'

'Stop calling me madam. It sounds so obscene.'

'Madam!'

'Call me Thilaka.' She dropped her voice. 'You look so cute when you are embarrassed.'

He hurriedly put down his cup, spilling some of the coffee, and got up to leave.

'Madam, this is so very inappropriate. I am a married man. Now I shall take my leave.'

He rushed down the stairs and thought he heard her laugh as he pushed his scooter out into the traffic.

'Ah, Professor Nilakantan. One moment if you may be so kind.'

Nilakantan looked up, wondering what Nallakannu wanted this time.

'Yes, yes. Please be seated.'

He closed the books he had arranged on the table, carefully inserting slips of paper to mark pages.

Proximity, familiarity, and a surplus of spare time meant that the faculty knew each others' foibles well. Each individual's quirks had been noticed and discussed threadbare. Thus, most of Nilakantan's colleagues knew that he didn't actually read the books that sat in a mound on his table. Once the suspicion that he was faking it got around, they had found ways of distracting him and changing the position of the page markers. He gave no indication of noticing any change. Ergo, his reading was an act for their benefit.

Nallakannu knew all this and waited patiently for Nilakantan to complete his ritual. Brahmins were picky about their rituals and Nilakantan was picky even by Brahminical standards.

'Yes. It is important for us to keep abreast of developments, Professor Nallakannu. The students of today expect no less. So I devote my spare time to the acquisition of knowledge.' He indicated the books.

'Indeed, professor. Such devotion to students is very heartening to see. Such devotion was the hallmark of ancient gurus and your efforts in this regard are very commendable. You are like a modern guru.'

'Thank you, professor.'

'Have you been able to investigate further the matter concerning contingent liabilities?'

'What contingent liabilities?'

'Last time, you were elucidating these details about

contingent liabilities. For the benefit of our Miss Dakshayini, if I am not mistaken.'

'What? Oh, yes, yes. Contingent liabilities. So many things going on, you see. Difficult business this, so many developments, so many changes. I have been busy with so many matters. But yes, my investigations are continuing. I have yet to reach definite conclusions, though.'

'Busy also with committee activities?'

'Oh that...you know, you were also there, there have been problems with the director.'

'So, the committee activities are at a standstill?'

'Yes and no.'

'Meaning?'

'You see, it is like this. Yes, because a committee's work never ends. Once we accept responsibility, we take this responsibility very seriously. We uncover facts, we do research, we improve our overall level of knowledge.'

'What facts have you uncovered?'

'Where can I even start? There is so much to learn, and what we don't know overwhelms what we know. This makes us humble. Modesty is a great virtue, as I am very fond of saying. In fact I tell my students this very fact and they greatly appreciate it. They tell me how modest I am. Of course I am very modest but I am always very happy to see this recognition by others. In fact, one student told me that I have so much to be modest about. Imagine, Professor Nallakannu, a student telling me all this, it actually brought tears to my eyes. One student even took out his handkerchief and said my tears were like Ganga *jalam*.'

'Yes, yes, but are you sure they were not pulling your leg?'

'What do you mean? If they and I are in so much agreement regarding modesty, how can you even suggest such a thing?'

'These students, they are very clever. Always trying to do funny things, so you should be very careful.'

'They did something in your class?'

Nallakannu leaned closer. 'I am telling you, and you only, this. One fellow, that Jagdeep from Meerut, he has this noise making programme on his phone. I was teaching one day and suddenly there was this big noise like...like...a gas discharge.'

'Bathroom gas discharge?'

'Indeed, but very loud. So I jumped up and had a gas discharge myself. A loud one, unfortunately. The bloody fools all started laughing. Only later was I able to ascertain the facts. In fact, it was Miss Dakshayini who pointed out. But at that moment, there was loud laughter from all the students.'

'Miss Dakshayini also?'

'No, no. She was busy taking notes as always. But to return to the point, you were saying that committee activities have come to a partial standstill. That is, if I understand you correctly.'

'Yes.'

'Yes?'

'Yes, that is what I said.'

'But...'

'See, it is a delicate situation. Like a fine balance. Clarifications are pending.'

'What clarifications?'

'That is what we also want to know. Pending the clarification of the clarifications which are pending, we are also pending.'

'Oh.'

Nilakantan knew when to lapse into silence. He sat back and crossed his arms. The silence was too much for Nallakannu.

'But you went to see the joint chancellor. Didn't he clarify what was pending?'

'No. We spoke. He listened. No clarifications forthcoming. Perhaps you could have come also and got the information firsthand.'

'What information?'

'Lack of information, that is what I am clarifying.'

'So, when might the next meeting of the committee be?'

'I am only a humble member of the committee. Chairman proposes, chairman disposes.'

Stalemate.

Not entirely reluctantly, Nallakannu unveiled his Brahmastra. 'The other day I saw something very strange.' He paused for effect.

Nilakantan was well aware, as were most of the faculty, of Nallakannu's deep insight into, and knowledge of, the assorted undercurrents that created the changing landscape of faculty solidarity and dissent.

'Strange?'

'Yes, indeed. This was something I was seeing for the first time.'

'Yes, yes?'

'Professor Thilaka.'

'Yes?'

'On a scooter.'

'Yes, yes?'

'With her hands around...'

'Yes, yes, yes...'

'Professor Sambandham.'

Shocked silence. Nallakannu leaned back, satisfied.

'She had her arms around Professor Sambandham?'

Nallakannu nodded. 'And,' he dropped his voice and their heads met, 'she was whispering in his ear.' A good sambhar needed the correct spices to taste right and Nallakannu had learned from experience that the same principle applied to gossip.

This was too much for Nilakantan. Logic dictated that if Thilaka had been whispering in Sambandham's ear, the reverse must have been true as well. He felt lightheaded and faint. A dozen possibilities, none satisfactory from his viewpoint, spun through his mind. For all the noise and posturing that constituted Thilaka's persona, she had a way about her, something well removed from the sullen obedience that was his lot at home, and he found that most attractive. Knowing her temper and her tongue, he pretended to loath her and kept his thoughts to himself, all the while hoping that someday she would recognize the look in his eye for what it was. And now, this.

The saga of the joint chancellor and the committee soon spilled out. Pleased with this happy outcome, Nallakannu left.

Negotiation Skills

A week off had restored some of the director's equanimity and erased the harsher recollections of the contretemps in his office and the meeting with the joint chancellor. He was able to look Jagan in the eye as he asked for the files that had accumulated in his absence. He knew that something needed to be done about the joint chancellor's most unreasonable demands and his time off had allowed him to give some thought as to what was to be done next.

He asked Jagan to summon Professor Agarwal.

Agarwal taught Human Capital Management.

Once, the subject was called Labour Management. Times changed, and with it the course title. His course became Industrial Relations. This morphed to a more politically correct Personnel Management. Agarwal's keen eye on the latest management trends meant a further titular updating, this time to Human Resource Management. A quarter century or so after his Labour Management days, AICTE stepped in to clean out old cob-webbed management notions. They brought in fresh thinking demanded by the twenty-first-century corporation. Thus, Human Resource Management became Human Capital Management.

The glitter of the packaging hid a more prosaic reality. Life was easier that way. Agarwal could now recite his course, from start to finish, from memory. Any question meant that the flow of words would stop, a mental rewinding to a point three paragraphs earlier would take place, and the stream of words would resume from that point. No further elaboration took place. The Factories Act of 1940 was the foundation on which the course was built and Agarwal's students from the 80s all the way to the first decade of the new century were proficient in the provisions of that Raj-era Act.

Unlike the others, Agarwal had a reason for his reluctance to modernize. Teaching took up only some of his time at the institute; revising his course had to take a back seat to other responsibilities. Agarwal guessed that these other responsibilities were the reason for the summons. It wasn't a bad trade-off, he thought to himself as he sat through the obligatory fifteen-minute wait in the director's ante-room.

Jagan eventually nodded, and Agarwal made his way into the sanctum sanctorum. Unlike some of his colleagues who were irritated at the petty delays associated with a directorial audience, Agarwal found comfort in these relaxing rituals. They were reminders that life meandered along at a sedate pace and that hurrying things along rarely helped.

'Ah, Professor Agarwal. All well with you I trust?'

'Yes, sir.' He was wary of these conversational gambits and gave as little away as possible.

'Very unfortunate, what happened here last week. We all have things we disagree about, but shouting and ransacking my office is no way to sort things out. Hartals and gheraos belong to the 70s and 80s. But, of course, you know all this.'

'Yes, sir.'

'Well, the reason I asked you to come is because there have been some disquieting developments.'

'Yes, sir.'

'You know...you see...your recruitment responsibilities...'

Agarwal didn't react. Better to wait for the director to come out with it. He stared blandly.

'Umm...last year, let us see...you were able to get us 55 students from, ah, your part of the country.'

'Yes, 55 from Meerut, Panipat and Kurukshetra. But also 17 from Bulandshahr and 8 from Ghaziabad, so 80 in total.'

'Yes, yes, of course.'

'And as I have already told you, it was extremely difficult, challenging even, getting students from UP and Haryana to Coimbatore.'

'Yes, of course, we are very appreciative of your efforts. Very appreciative indeed. Now the joint chancellor and I have had a review meeting, um, discussing our intake for the coming year.'

'Yes, sir.'

'You see, despite our best efforts, we could only get 192 students, against our sanctioned 250. The joint chancellor strongly feels that...well, he expressed his desire...that he would like to see a full contingent of students.'

Agarwal could see what was coming and said nothing.

'Ah...umm...there are distinct challenges, shall we say. I mean, given last year's experience. So, what I mean to say is, understanding of course that this will be difficult and asking a lot from you, would it be possible for you to generate...I mean recruit, of course...say 150 students this year?'

Silence, as the number was chewed on and digested.

'I mean, of course, 150 from *your* catchment areas... as you say, UP and Haryana...'

Silence once more, this time as a bargaining ploy.

'I understand the difficulties, that goes without saying, of course, and I suspect that all of this is a bit unexpected. But our budget...we are in a difficult position and the joint chancellor is very keen... If you get my meaning...'

'Last year, as I told you, I faced many difficulties. It took so much time, I had to spend from my own pocket to explain to the parents about Sundarambal Institute, about Coimbatore. In fact, it was such an effort for them to even pronounce Sundarambal and Coimbatore. You see, they all think that South India means Madras and Bangalore, and that South Indians eat only idli and sambhar. No tinda, no lauki, no dal, no chappati, they ask me how their children are going to eat and enjoy good health with dosa and idli only.'

'Well, you were compensated generously for your efforts, and the joint chancellor himself was most appreciative of your efforts, most appreciative indeed.'

'Director sahib, 50,000 per student was not bad, not a small sum. I am not complaining, but to get 150? Such difficulties I faced for 80. In Bulandshahr and these other western UP towns, it was such a problem even to meet a student. And the parents, baap re... Director sahib, you are sitting here in a nice AC office and all, you should come with me to see Bulandshahr, real western UP town. You will never understand the people there. Last year one boy, his parents told me, you want to take my boy to Madras and Bangalore and all, *you* pay *us* money. Imagine, sahib, we are providing education and *they* are asking money! Another problem. They are all asking, what job is my son getting? We are paying all this money, sending to Madras and Bangalore, and then what? I don't want this fellow coming back with MBA and watching TV at home. Getting MBA, these fellows become fancy, they don't want to work in the fields anymore. Meerut University is sufficient for that. But, director sahib, what jobs *are* our students getting? What can I tell these parents? And, next year, these 80 will be telling their friends that professors Agarwal and Sambandham and all are excellent professors, but good jobs, that Sundarambal Institute is not getting us. There is justice in the parents' questions, director sahib.'

'Okay, 60,000 then.'

'Director sahib, what is this you are saying? Prices of vegetables are going up. Petrol for my scooter, up. Rent for my flat, up. Wife is always complaining, saying Agarwalji, why did you bring me to this place? Coimbatore is a very costly city compared to Meerut. And all this in addition to all those other difficulties. Sixty thousand? Better that I teach instead. Maybe an executive development course for Coimbatore industry executives. I'm sure they will appreciate my rich experience and advanced teaching methods.'

The director shuddered at the thought of unleashing his faculty on the Coimbatore industrialists.

'What do you have in mind, then? You must appreciate the constraints I am under.'

'Director sahib, that is not for me to say. I am just an employee. How can I even suggest...'

'Seventy thousand.'

'These are difficult times, with inflation and all. Eighty thousand, Director sahib.'

'Seventy-five thousand.'

Agarwal sighed. 'For the sake of our institute and given your appeal about the budget, okay. I am also thinking of the many students who will benefit from the education here. Who am I to deny them?'

Relieved that he had concluded the negotiations at an acceptable cost, the director turned his attention to the files. Sitting on top was a large envelope, its corners smeared with kum-kum and sandalwood paste, addressed to Thiru director. Mildly annoyed at getting what appeared to be a wedding invitation sent to his office, he tore it open.

Office of the Joint Chancellor
Sundarambal University
Coimbatore, Tamil Nadu
(Approved as a Deemed to be University under Section 3, UGC Act)

2nd April 2011

The Director
Sundarambal Institute of Management

Dear Thiru Director,
I have been asked to communicate the decisions of the Honourable Chancellor, Sundarambal University, Dr A. Rakshasan, BA, BL, D.Litt., MP, as follows:

1. The Chancellor is willing to accept the honorary doctorate offered by the Sundarambal Institute of Management. He has indicated that 18th April, 24th April and 2nd May are suitable dates for the special convocation to be held for this purpose. The President of India, the Prime Minister of India, the President of America and the Chief Minister of Tamil Nadu are acceptable to him as chief guests. Kindly revert with confirmation of the date and the chief guest for this august occasion. You are also requested to make all arrangements for the same.
2. The Chancellor has accorded his consent for a compulsory course entitled 'Management Actions of Dr A. Rakshasan, BA, BL, D.Litt., MP' for the

MBA students of the Sundarambal Institute of Management. A senior faculty member may kindly be deputed to finalize details of the course with Thiru P.K. Chandramouleeshwaran, Personal Assistant to Dr A. Rakshasan, BA, BL, D.Litt., MP, Chancellor, Sundarambal University (Approved as a Deemed to be University under Section 3, UGC Act).

3. The Chancellor has directed you to eliminate the rats in your canteen using Rat Kill™ manufactured by Sundarambal Industries (Dr A. Rakshasan, BA, BL, D.Litt., MP, sole prop.). The Chancellor has kindly consented to offer a 5% (five per cent only) discount on the price of Rat Kill™. You may contact Thiru P.K. Chandramouleeshwaran, Personal Assistant to Dr A. Rakshasan, BA, BL, D.Litt., MP, Chancellor, Sundarambal University (Approved as a Deemed to be University under Section 3, UGC Act) to avail of the same. The Joint Chancellor's office may kindly be informed following successful elimination of the aforementioned rats.

Kindly acknowledge receipt of this letter. The Joint Chancellor's office may kindly be kept informed of progress on all these matters.

Yours sincerely,
B. Kumbhakarnan
Joint Chancellor
Sundarambal University

The director read the letter twice. He ran his tongue over his lips. This was a joke. Surely this had to be a joke. This was ridiculous. Someone was trying to pull one over him.

'Jagan, come in here.'

'Yes, sir.'

'Do you remember this letter?' He waved the sandal-pasted cover at Jagan.

'Yes, sir.'

'Where did it come from?'

'Personally delivered by the joint chancellor's PA. I signed the receipt for it. You were away on sick leave when it came, sir.'

The director swallowed hard.

'Okay. Thank you, Jagan.'

'Any further instructions, sir?'

'That will be all. Thank you.'

Oh my God, he thought to himself as he sank into his chair. Where did *this* come from? What on earth? Who the hell? What the…? One week off, equanimity barely restored, life barely settled into an even keel – and all the while, someone, some bloody group… This couldn't be the joint chancellor's handiwork. The man was barely capable of thought, for heaven's sake. If he could just find out who…

He leaned on his table, head in hand, rocking back and forth the way he usually did when under extreme stress. There was nothing he could do. Even if he did find out, it would make no bloody difference. They had gone behind his back. God only knew what they had told that incompetent fool. Kumbhakarnan indeed!

'Jagan, could you call Professor Agarwal again?'

Dark thoughts, depressing thoughts, feelings of impotent rage, of victimhood, all crossed his fevered mind. A sense of complete loneliness, of being surrounded and buffeted by hostile forces intent on a long-drawn-out and public humiliation, of being a barely flickering candle in a desolate sea of darkness, came over him. He sank even lower into his chair. He was middle-aged now, there was nowhere left to go. There were no friends he could call on, there would be little sympathy on offer from his family. Darkness. Oblivion. Curtains.

'Sir, you called me?'

He floated up from some deep well of misery.

'Yes. Yes. Professor Agarwal, thank you for coming.'

'You called. In response to your call only I came.'

Call. *The Call of the Wild. White Fang.* Jack London.

'What? Oh, yes. Yes.'

Agarwal could see a letter before the director. He couldn't read it without making his intentions too obvious. He would have to wait to learn just why the director was acting so strangely. Grateful for being able to earn some of his salary sitting in silence in the director's office, he waited.

'Ah. Well. Professor Agarwal, what we have to discuss is in strict confidence. We have...ah...come to understandings, private understandings, details of which have never left this room. I am...uh...grateful for the discretion you have already maintained about these matters and would be very grateful for more of the same.'

'Yes, sir.'

'It is like this. Would you by any chance know anything about an honorary doctorate being suggested for our chancellor?'

'No, sir,' lied Agarwal.

'Hmm. Or a special course of some kind suggested by faculty?'

'It is my understanding, sir, that you were to constitute a committee to examine ideas of Thiruvalluvarji and Periyarji in respect of management. However, I may be mistaken.'

'No, no, I mean no, you are not mistaken, there were some suggestions along those lines. My motto in such cases is: act in haste, repent at leisure. This is not, of course, to suggest that these were bad suggestions. It is always good to see the faculty on the lookout for fresh ideas and innovations in the way we teach. But we need to examine these suggestions from every angle, hold them up to the light, so to speak. A thorough appraisal does no one any harm, I always say. But that is not what I had in mind. Was there anything else, any other special course that might have been floated as a trial balloon by anyone?'

'Balloons are not allowed on campus. Joint chancellor's orders.'

'No, no, that's not what I meant, for heaven's sake. I meant, suggestions for any other special courses, you know, any discussions you might have overheard in the canteen?'

A pause, indicative of deep thought.

'Directorji, one thing I am thinking.'

'Yes?'

'Our earlier discussions. A hundred and fifty students you were mentioning.'

'Of course. We had shaken hands on 75,000.'

'I was thinking, 150 is a very challenging number. Very, very challenging.'

'I'm sure you had given that due thought before shaking hands on 75,000.'

Agarwal looked pained. 'You see, directorji, between then and now I have been doing calculations. So many expenses I will have to incur, travel, tea–coffee–samosas for parents, other expenses also. Bulandshahr, maybe 10 students, maybe 15. Then I have to go to the next town. Travel, hotels, information on eligible students... These study centres are all only interested in making money. Welfare of students, good advice, all of that is completely absent. You want ten names? Money. Ten more? More money. These days they are talking about inflation rates, prices of onions and potatoes, petrol and kerosene. Terrible, only money. What am I to do? Government policy, economic policy, budget all resulting in higher expenses.'

'But 75,000 per student should adequately compensate you for your expenses. After all, it is a significant increase over the last year. I too have a P&L that I am responsible for.'

'P&L? L&T I am hearing about and also P&T but I am not understanding this P&L.'

'Profit and loss. Surely, professor, you must know this. You are teaching in a business school!' He tried his best to keep his disgust hidden. Really, this lot was beyond redemption.

'Oh, *that* P&L. Yes, of course I know, not to worry. But I also know that last year my 80 students added to your P and not to L. This year my 150 also will be adding to your P. To P or not to P, that is the question in my humble opinion. Two daughters I have. L only. Marriage costs? L. School costs? L. Gold jewellery? L also. All L and no P in my life. And expenses for getting the 150? Even more L. Tell me, directorji, what am I to do? I have no interest in money. I am interested only in helping students. To me the teaching profession is a noble profession.'

'Okay. Five thousand per student as additional expenses. No more. Now, that other matter we were discussing?'

'That, director sir, I have no information about.'

Organizational Behaviour II

'Thiru director?'

'Yes, sir.'

'You have got letter addressed to yourself?'

'Yes, sir. I wanted to…'

'Chancellor wants to convey that 50,000 of his followers have expressed desire to witness the honorary doctorate ceremony. You were asked to make suitable arrangements. Which date have you chosen?'

'Second May, sir.' He was up shit creek without a paddle and choosing the last possible day would allow some wiggle room.

'Chancellor has been informed?'

'I was in the process of drafting a letter…'

'Only in the process? First, all these faculty committees. Now in the process of drafting. Thiru director, when do you actually work?'

'That is not entirely fair, sir. All matters are being attended to. You have my assurance that…'

'Yes, yes. Assurances are very nice, but actions are essential. Action, not words. The chancellor's words, not mine. Thiru Chandramouleeshwaran is to be kept informed of the programme of action on all matters, copy to me. In addition, the chancellor has expressed his humble desire to deliver the first lecture of the management action course to all Sundarambal students. The chancellor's followers have also expressed their desire to listen to the lecture. The chancellor is also thinking that many people throughout the world – in America, Russia and England, also China, Japan, Singapore and Malaysia – where chancellor has followers, will want to listen to his lecture on this management subject. So, the chancellor is thinking, why not broadcast the lecture on the Sundarambal TV network? Not his idea, of course, but his followers are all saying, why are we not getting this lecture? So, you take action on that also. Thiru Chandramouleeshwaran will be calling to ascertain details. Copy me on all matters, of course.'

Words failed the director. So did thoughts. So did everything else that might have marked him out as a functioning member of an intelligent species. He went blank. A handful of seconds ticked by, then a full minute.

'Thiru director? Are you listening?'

'Er...yes, sir.'

'Then why are you not acknowledging this important message that I have been conveying? Here I am shouting like a dog...no, like a wolf...no, when a wolf shouts other wolves reply. This I myself have heard in Valparai. Very frightening, hearing this wolf shouting in the middle of the night and all the other wolves replying. So I send my PA to go and shoot all the wolves. Silly fellow killed the watchman's dog by mistake. So I am not shouting like a wolf. But Buddha, many questions he is asking God and God is taking many years to reply. So you think you are God, Thiru director?'

'Of course not, sir,' replied the director, by now thoroughly bewildered.

'Then why are you not replying?'

'I was just thinking about a suitable plan of action encompassing all your instructions.'

'Thinking, thinking, thinking. Never doing. That is your problem, Thiru director. Always talking, always thinking, never working. Now I'm telling you very clearly, chancellor says, do, don't think. Like that, I also do. Thinking is a complete waste of time. That is my advice to you. Now don't forget anything I have been saying. And remember that watchman's dog.'

It took the director more than a few seconds to realize that the joint chancellor had rung off. His mind was still ringing from the cacophonous outburst. Some part of his thinking harked back to Drucker, Peters, Ghosal. Thinkers all, they had come up with deep insights into management and managers. And here was this uncouth son of a bitch, prime beneficiary of Nepotism Incorporated, telling him not to think. Resignation? Not an option. His wife had made it amply clear during his week off that his presence at home during working hours was not appreciated. He was not on talking terms with his sons. His bank balance did not reflect his years of toil. His age and years away from the corporate world, not to mention his Sundarambal association meant a substantial diminution of his career prospects. He was boxed in.

'Jagan?' His voice carried all the weight of his years and thoughts. 'Please get me Mr Chandramouleeshwaran. He is the chancellor's PA.'

Keeping track of the comings and goings of Dr A. Rakshasan, BA, BL, D.Litt., MP, was P.K. Chandramouleeshwaran, a Brahmin whose disdain for his boss's antecedents took second place to his awareness of the potential inherent in his position.

P.K., as he was known, was a short, fat, oily man whose appearance and garb belied his influence and wealth. He had realized early on that Rakshasan was one of life's winners. He also came to know that Rakshasan's success had something to do with his not trusting the vagaries of the legal system when it came to commercial disputes. Sickles and knives had given way to Heckler and Koch as his preferred dispute resolution tool as he moved up in life. P.K. was an intelligent man with strong self-preservation instincts. It was amply clear to him that crossing, double-crossing or otherwise interfering with Rakshasan's progress was not conducive to continued good health. So he made sure that he did nothing that could be construed as disloyalty. All attempts at influencing him were dutifully reported to his boss and the latter's generosity in settling for a reasonable split of his business proceeds bought him absolute loyalty.

P.K. was servile when it came to his boss. He expected servility when others came to him. Seated behind a large desk and an array of cell phones arranged in order of importance, he barked out impatient orders which were then followed up by one of a dozen assistant PAs. These assistants to the personal assistant (APAs) themselves constituted a hierarchy. APA 12 dealt with matters deemed too unimportant for APAs 1 to 11.

Those who had dealt with P.K. knew that return calls meant trouble. They also knew that dealing directly with him was a privilege of sorts, but this insight was vouchsafed only to those in the know.

The director was not part of this inner circle. He soon realized that P.K. was unlike anyone he had ever dealt with.

'Could I speak to Mr Chandramouleeshwaran, please?'

'Sir busy. Call later.'

'This is the director of the Sundarambal Institute of Management. The joint chancellor, Mr Kumbhakarnan, requested me to contact Mr Chandramouleeshwaran. I'll hold on until he is free.'

He held on for a few moments before realizing that he had been cut off.

'Jagan, I asked you to connect me to Mr Chandramouleeshwaran, not his PA.'

'Not possible, sir.'

'Why not?'

'Technical difficulties.'

'What do you mean?'

'P.K. sir answering only chancellor's phone. All other calls APAs answer.'

'Well, could you ask to hold on until he is free? You can then connect me.'

'Not possible, sir.'

'Why not, for heaven's sake.'

'P.K. sir speaks only when he is ready. Disturbing P.K. sir means very big disturbance. I am not recommending, that is my humble advice, sir.'

'Have you ever spoken to Mr Chandramouleeshwaran, then?'

Jagan snorted with laughter. 'Me, sir? You are making a big joke about me, sir. P.K. sir is a very big person. I am only a director's PA. How can my humble self talk to P.K. sir?'

'Oh, well. Keep trying.'

Contact was finally established three hours later. The director was his usual courteous self.

'Mr Chandramouleeshwaran? This is the director of the Sundarambal Institute of Management. I was requested by...'

'Kovai institute function, no? Date? You have not informed date.'

'Oh, yes. As I was discussing with...'

'Date?'

'The joint chancellor and I discussed this matter and decided that the second of May...'

'Confirmed?'

'I beg your pardon?'

'Is second May confirmed?'

'Yes, but…'

'Function at 11 a.m. One hour function, Leader will be speaking for 45 minutes. Chief guest?'

'I beg your pardon?'

'Who is chief guest? Leader is wanting to know.'

'We have contacted the CM's office and the PMO, but have yet to receive a response.'

'What? No chief guest for Leader's important function?'

'We are trying our best…'

'Kindly ascertain identity of chief guest and revert at the earliest. This is of utmost importance. Following matters are to be attended to. Transportation of Leader's followers. Contact Sundarambal Transport Corporation for the needful. Facilities for rest and nuisance. Food and drink to be provided. Biryani, beer and brandy may be provided. Orders may kindly be placed with Sundarambal Distilleries. Ample quantities for ample followers. Sundarambal TV to be provided adequate facilities for broadcast. Leader has kindly agreed to followers' request for press conference. Kindly ensure representation from national and international press. Leader will be speaking in Tamil on this auspicious occasion and also to students. Translation service will be needed for the national and international audience. Suitable arrangements to be made for Leader's arrival and departure. My assistant Arogyasami will be in touch regarding timely and satisfactory completion of arrangements.'

He hung up abruptly. No social niceties, no acknowledgment of the director's status, nothing. Arogyasami was APA 8. Without his knowing it, the director had been consigned to the bottom half of the Sundarambal empire.

The director now scrambled to put down everything P.K. had said. Thoughts, feelings and a full awareness of his situation all waited off stage until he was done, then they came on in an overwhelming rush. Dry-mouthed, he slumped in his chair as the enormity of the tasks facing him became clear.

Corporate Social Responsibility

'Sir?'

Sambandham looked up. It was that cursed Dakshayini.

'Could I take a few moments of your time, sir?'

He had not graded anything since that last fiasco, and the somnolent tenor of his classes had continued uninterrupted. Therefore, he couldn't quite understand what this pestilential girl wanted. Aware that his continued employment owed something to the rather substantial fees paid by the students, and unable to come up with an excuse at short notice, he ill-humouredly beckoned her in.

'Sir, this is about the essay on corporate social responsibility that you assigned us.'

His heart sank, his head nodded automatically, he braced himself for what was coming.

'Some of us have been discussing the topic, sir, as part of our Business Issues Club. We see that there are a number of nuances whose ultimate implications are not always clear. We have tried reading up on it but find ourselves confused by some of the statements made.

We would like to organize a conference on corporate social responsibility with both industry speakers and professors. Both real-life issues on the implementation of CSR and the latest thinking on the subject could be covered. We need a faculty member to guide us, sir. Will you help us?'

Sambandham hated being put on the spot. The spot, though, had been successfully pursuing him from his early childhood. Now it had him in its sights once more. He stared malevolently at her. There was a doe-like innocence to her which was impervious to his thoughts and she looked back at him eagerly. He sighed. Thilaka, Anbuchezian, Agarwal, Nilakantan, all the others, all with nothing better to do than to plot silly games against that fool director – all of them to choose from, and she had come to him.

'What do you want me to do? I am very busy as the chairman of the AICTE committee. The director himself has entrusted this heavy responsibility to me. I have so many issues to consider and deal with, deadlines and all.'

'Sir, I know we are asking you to take a few precious minutes out of your busy schedule. But all we are looking for is a faculty advisor. We are planning to write a white paper on the subject and put together a list of topics to be covered in the conference along with a list of potential invitees. Only then will we ask you for your advice and suggestions. Sir, the director might not agree to a conference without a faculty advisor approving the conference programme. In addition, potential sponsors will be taking a hard look at the conference programme before committing themselves. We need your guidance and advice for all this.Can we count on you, sir?'

Put like that, he could hardly say no. She could be charming when she wasn't hounding him about her grades. There was also the possibility of incorporating some of that white paper into something bearing his name. The director was always going on about research and publications. Potential bonuses, thus far unclaimed, had been dangled before the faculty and here was an opportunity to grab something for himself. There was also the possibility that this could end up being his ticket out of the institute and onto something bigger and better. A publication in some newspaper, perhaps, that could even lead to some conference invites; maybe some consulting assignments as well. He would, of course, take along Dakshayini as co-author. Never deny credit where it was due. She was a bright girl; they might well end up discussing management over dinner. And then?

He shook his head, attempting to stop his thoughts from barrelling down down strangely enticing paths. He was Sambandham, married to Mrs Sambandham, and Dakshayini was young enough to be his daughter. He put on his grade A professorial air.

'I'll need to see your white paper first. Then, upon satisfactory perusal, I can approve.'

'Thank you, sir. Thank you very much, sir. We will write up the white paper and get back to you, sir.'

Sambandham nodded sagely. If nothing else, the 'research paper' portion of his thoughts was something that he could realistically look forward to.

Sambandham turned the pages slowly. Dakshayini sat waiting. She had to think that he *was* reading it, so he nodded thoughtfully, pursed his lips and frowned, but not all at once. He stared at the wall before turning each page. Every now and then he stared at her meaningfully. She *was* rather pretty and if he was going to get into trouble with his wife, better a few moments with her than that ghastly Thilaka. He glanced up: she was looking at him. He nodded contentedly.

He reached the end and made a show of going through the whole thing again. Twelve pages, closely spaced, followed by a long list of references. Impressive.

'Some good points you have made here,' he said finally.

'Thank you, sir,' she said.

'I need to read this in detail. You see, organizing a conference is a serious business. Topics to be covered require lots of thought. A proper structure is needed.' He tried to think of something more to say and came up blank. 'So I need to go through this in detail. In detail. To check the topics. Structure also.'

'Does it look okay otherwise, sir?'

Did she have to look at him like this? 'Hmm, yes, okay, but a detailed evaluation is required. That I shall do. I shall revert in a few days.'

'Thank you, sir. Shall I check with you in two or three days?'

'Little longer. A detailed evaluation takes time, you see. One week minimum. I also have other onerous responsibilities, committee responsibilities and so forth. The director has appointed me chairman of AICTE committee, as I have already told you. Serious deliberations are taking place therein. But the welfare of students is also important. So it will take time. But all good things happen in good time. Hence, one week minimum.'

Dakshayini left after some more effusive thank yous and Sambandham settled down to actually read what she had given him. There was no doubt that it was well written. What it really meant, he could not tell, and after two pages he gave up. He flipped through the pages once more. There were paradoxes, conundrums, shareholder rights, environmental impacts, social accounting standards, SRKs and much else. There were footnotes, copious references and a tentative conference schedule. There was a list of outstanding and contentious issues. All in all, well removed from anything he had encountered in his academic career. Time to dust off Wren and Martin. But then, maybe not. He wasn't going to understand anything anyway. Better to just think of that smile and wonder why she had chosen him, since in reality he had little to contribute by way of advice.

'Did it!' Dakshayini giggled excitedly.

'He read it?'

'Pretended to read through it once. God, he's so bad at pretending.'

'He looked at you?'

More giggles. 'Couldn't keep his eyes off me. It was so creepy. Pretend to read, pretend not to stare at me. Pretend to read, pretend not to stare at me. I thought I was going to burst out laughing. Gosh, I'm supposed to be mugging hard for the finals. If Ma hears what I've been doing she will kill me. Anyway, you told me I'd never have the guts. Now that I did it, where's my treat?'

'No, not yet. The bet was that he will agree to chair the conference.'

'Come on, that's not fair. I told you he wouldn't notice those bits about SRK.'

'You said he pretended to read. So you don't really know that he didn't notice. Conference, then we'll give you a proper treat.'

'Chhee, I have to wait for a week. So boring.'

The Law of Unintended Consequences

The letter from AICTE was an unwelcome interruption. Between P.K., the joint chancellor, Arogyasami and, providing context to their many discussions, Dr Rakshasan himself, AICTE's imminent visit had slipped the director's mind.

Now, it seemed, there were two additional members of the visiting party. Two IAS officers. What on earth would they do? And how was he to 'negotiate' those additional seats with these worthies in attendance? Even worse, they had juggled their dates around and were proposing second May as the date for their inspection. Damn! He needed to urgently suggest some other date, any date really other than the second. Not that they would listen, they never did, the bastards.

More to the point, had Sambandham and his noisy and ineffectual colleagues sorted out those inconsequential lacunae that had so exercised the fine minds at AICTE? What was the point of having these jokers as the faculty if they could not be depended upon for anything? Why had he even asked them to accept this responsibility? The sense of being boxed in by incompetent mediocrity was overwhelming.

He asked Jagan to summon Sambandham.

The director waited impatiently: Sambandham appeared to be taking more time than was needed. These people were supposed to be management faculty, for heaven's sake, and instead behaved like clerical staff in some musty government office.

He heard voices in the ante-room, the sounds of an argument.

An obviously upset Jagan called on the intercom. 'All AICTE committee faculty here, sir. No Professor Sambandham only, all coming they are saying.'

'What? I thought I asked you to only call Professor Sambandham.'

'Yes, yes, that is what I did, but everyone came without asking. Now they are saying that they all are coming.'

'Okay, let them in.'

The committee trooped in. Their entry lacked the drama of their previous appearance. High emotion had been replaced by a sullen determination. The committee chairman came in mid-pack and tried to avoid eye contact.

'Well, Professor Sambandham, what has been the progress in attending to the so-called lacunae pointed out by AICTE? Might I remind you that we don't have much time before they visit? I've heard in addition that two senior bureaucrats from the ministry will be accompanying the team. It appears, therefore, that the inspection will be a thorough one. Where do we stand?'

'We are all standing here,' said Nilakantan.

The director sighed and tried not to show his exasperation. 'Professor Nilakantan, that was not what I meant. Are we prepared for their inspection? Have we made the changes indicated by them?'

'We the AICTE committee had clearly expressed our unhappiness over having to clear up the consequences resulting from the recommendations of another committee constituted by you without consulting the faculty body. This committee continues to hold the opinion that, for this reason, the terms of reference wherein this committee was constituted are unacceptable to it.'

Thilaka had been anointed the designated speaker given her ways with the English language. She now turned to her colleagues, who nodded vigorously in agreement. Sambandham alone had the mien of a trapped rat and tried to split the difference between faculty solidarity and deference to authority.

'This was conveyed very clearly to you before our mala fide expulsion from your office. It is this committee's contention that given the serious and unresolved questions about its constitution, it cannot be expected to address any of the issues assigned to it until the impugnments are mutually resolved.'

The director gaped at her. 'You mean...'

'We have resolved not to address any of the alleged lacunae until and unless our primary grievances are satisfactorily addressed.'

'You mean you have done nothing as far as the AICTE letter is concerned?'

'Affirmative,' replied Thilaka, taking a cue from the American action serials she and her son were addicted to.

'This is ridiculous. I mean, you all know that the inspection group is due. Professor Sambandham, I made it clear to you that the dates of the surprise visits were no surprise. All of you know the consequences of de-recognition. And yet I find that you have chosen to sit tight…'

'We are all standing here,' said Nilakantan.

The director took a few deep breaths. 'I'm aware of that, Professor Nilakantan. God has been generous enough to give me eyes and I can clearly see you standing. I was metaphorically referring to this committee's refusal to take action on a very urgent matter which has the potential to put all our students' careers in jeopardy.'

'Professor Anbuchezian and myself, we have made important suggestions, namely exposure of students to revered thoughts of Periyar and Thiruvalluvar. Can I enquire into the status of these suggestions?'

'Whose fault is this anyway?' Thilaka was back on the attack. 'Who called in the security when we were having a discussion earlier?'

'Jagan did,' said the director involuntarily.

'And who employed Jagan? Malathi madam very good secretary. Treated faculty with respect. Therefore security intrusions are your responsibility.' Sambandham, sensing the straws in the wind, felt emboldened to contribute to the discussion.

'Indeed,' continued Thilaka. 'Any constituted committee has a well-defined mandate. Any change in that mandate without prior consultation and approval means that the committee is ipso facto null and void. Therefore, logically and legally, this committee no longer exists. It follows that continuing this discussion is a waste of our collective time. Gentlemen, there is nothing further to discuss. Let's go.'

'But...but...you, you were given a responsibility.'

'Constitute another committee. Or get your green committee to clean up the mess they have left behind. We shall be taking legal advice regarding the scope of our faculty duties. Good day.'

They marched out solemnly.

The green committee. In an effort to sensitize students to environmental concerns, he had asked the first years to form groups and come up with suggestions for a 'greener' campus.

One group had suggested giving away all the battery-powered clocks – 'batteries are harmful to the environment, sir' – and replacing them with sundials. The many flagpoles and statues of the chancellor around the campus could be used for this and, taking the Jantar Mantar as inspiration, the calibrated dials could double as slides for the pre-primary children of the Sundarambal Matriculation School elsewhere on the campus.

Another had taken its remit literally. After an extensive survey of paints, they had recommended a particularly hideous shade of green for all the buildings.

A third had come up with a blueprint for a modern bullock cart which would take care of all campus transportation needs. The bullock droppings would serve as fuel for gobar gas plants situated around the campus.

The only sensible suggestions had been from the group which had studied the canteen and come up with some ideas for saving energy. Relieved that there was at least one diamond in the rough, and wanting to encourage continued out-of-the-box thinking, those ideas had been put to work.

Trust the faculty to turn this into a case of the law of unintended consequences.

'The AICTE committee met with the director.' Sambandham, mindful of his wife's lack of interest in his professional life, normally kept a wary distance from her. The times when she was in the kitchen were the most sensitive: he was well aware of her resentment at having to feed a husband whose virtues had been oversold, and maintained a safe and silent barrier devoid of any sort of provocation.

The day's events had been noteworthy, though. It wasn't every day that they got to confront the director in his lair. Even rarer were the days when they got the better of him. Come to think of it, it had never happened before. Most of all, though, he still felt a glow remembering his role in the proceedings. He had spoken up, spoken clearly, and articulated in no uncertain terms the committee's consensus. A rare occurrence this, his progress from being a wallflower to committee spokesman – something else that had never happened before. In that glow, Dakshayini's asking him to be faculty advisor took on a new meaning, an added significance. He, Sambandham, was at last being taken seriously. This was big news, something he couldn't just keep to himself. He needed to tell someone about it, even if his wife was the only one on hand and in the kitchen at that.

Something, a fleeting expression not suggestive of his being the deliverer of glad tidings, crossed her face and Sambandham took a precautionary step back. She looked up from the pot of simmering rasam and wiped sweat off her brow. Her hand clenched the ladle suggestively. Things did not look promising and Sambandham took another step back.

'Who was that woman?'

'What?'

'Are you deaf? Who was that woman?'

'Which woman?'

'I was told that you were going around with a fat woman on your scooter. First I didn't believe, then I'm being given address, so I am waiting and there you are getting down with this fat woman and going into her flat and all. And here I am cooking rasam and sambhar and poriyal in this hot kitchen for you. For a useless husband who takes a fat woman around on a scooter? Why?'

He ducked as the ladle, full of hot rasam, flew towards him. Thoughts flew, gathered coherence, settled uneasily. Today had been the second time. As before, Thilaka's scooter was at the workshop. As before, the words which would have allowed him to escape remained elusive, and words had failed him even when she invited him up for coffee again. Dazzled by her green sari (silver sequins thrown in for free) he had not noticed his wife lurking around.

'She is a married woman,' he blurted out.

'What? Shameless rascal! Scoundrel! You have the guts to tell me that you are meeting a married fat woman! My life was ruined the day I met you. All this cooking I am doing for you. And what do you do? You fool around with this fat woman, shamelessly going around town on a scooter.'

'She is not that fat,' escaped his lips involuntarily.

'Fool! Donkey! Buffalo! To think that I am supposed to respect you as a husband! Not fat? She is fatter than an elephant's backside. And after everything I've done for you all these years, you run after a cross between a buffalo and a pregnant elephant. What do I do now?' She burst into tears.

'I think the rasam is boiling over.'

Wrong choice of words. She came charging at him in a blind, tear-crazed fury. He scuttled behind the sofa, weaving back and forth to avoid her blows.

'She only gave me some coffee. Her scooter had gone for servicing. I think she even has a son.'

'Does she have a husband?'

'How would I know? Since she has a son she must have a husband as well.'

'See. You are cleverly meeting her when her husband is away. I knew you were up to no good.'

'No, no, I am telling you, two times her scooter has gone for service, two times she has asked for lift.'

'And she puts her arm around you like some actress?'

'Maybe she didn't want to fall off.'

'How many years we have been married? More than twenty? How many times I have put my arm around you?'

He didn't need to think hard. In fact, they kept as much distance between them as the scooter's seat would allow. 'Never,' he mumbled.

'How many times have I fallen off the scooter?'

Silence.

'See, I am a respectable person from a good family. Never will I put my arm around a man, not even my husband. Not like that slut. Who does she think she is? Some big actress? Tell her that women with the backside of a pregnant elephant can never become an actress. And no more meals for you in this house. You can take your bedding and sleep on the floor outside.'

She stormed back into the kitchen to tend to what was left of the rasam. Stunned, Sambandham wondered what was happening to him. First the director, now his wife. Life was denying him even the smallest of pleasures.

A thought struck him as he swatted away the swarming mosquitoes and drifted uneasily towards sleep: Someone had told his wife about his scooter rides with Thilaka. But who? And why?

She burst into tears as soon as she saw him. Behind her, his arms gesticulating helplessly, his face seeking forgiveness for being unable to do anything about it, stood Jagan.

The director quickly put away his crossword and tried to assume an air of directorial busyness. The flood of tears continued unabated for a few minutes, punctuated only by loud wails and heart-wrenching appeals to various gods. Directorial busyness soon gave way to an appalled curiosity. Who was this woman? Had he seen her before? Jagan's helpless shrug conveyed nothing. The tears of Tamil women have always reduced fearsome Tamil men to silence, and Jagan's futile attempts at explanation proved stillborn.

Possible explanations rushed through the director's mind. A parent upset that her child had been failed? The institute treated its students as valued customers; failing them was not an option given to faculty. A student suspended for some minor violation of one of the joint chancellor's sillier rules? He didn't remember any such episode in the recent past. A boy talking to her daughter? Now *that* was a possibility. Which girl? Was this Dakshayini's mother, here to express her concern about the baleful influence of the institute's boys on her daughter's grades? Worse, were the boys exercising their baleful influence on her *heart*? Even worse, were *North Indian* boys exercising their baleful influence on her chaste South Indian heart?

He cleared his throat, searching for words that would calm the fevered imaginings of Dakshayini's mother.

Sniffles and tears done with, the lady finally spoke. 'Myself Swapnasundari. Wife of Thiru Sambandham, faculty member of your good institute.'

Having followed his thoughts down one path, the director allowed logic to take him to the obvious conclusion. That two-faced little runt! Of all people! How had that sweet and sensible girl allowed a nondescript timeserver to steal her heart? How on earth was he going to deal with this woman? And, worse, how was he going to deal with Dakshayini's mother when she showed up, rolling pin in hand? Above all, what had Sambandham got that he, the director and the only one with intellect, words and personality, didn't have? Life had been delivering its share of knocks; this in some ways hurt most of all.

'Madam,' he began, measuring out his words even as his thoughts ran wild.

'This person, this Mrs Thilakavathi, she is seducing my husband. What sort of institute are you running? Is this an institute or a house of ill repute?'

'Madam, what are you saying? Are you referring to Professor Thilakavathi?'

'I'm telling you, that woman Thilakavathi, your staff, married with son also, is seducing my husband. You are allowing all this under your nose. What are you going to do about it?'

The director gave an audible sigh of relief that the virginal Dakshayini remained unsullied by Sambandham's insidious ways. Maybe the day wasn't such a bad one, after all. A sniffle from across the desk reminded him that the day wasn't done with him yet. The woman was clearly distraught and was expecting him to sort out her marital problems and stem the flow of tears. She was unlikely to be amenable to reason. The thought of Thilakavathi and Sambandham was bizarre enough to justify a snort or two of laughter. Just what was it with Sambandham? All these years hidden out of sight and now here he was, leading faculty dissent and behaving like some middle-aged Lothario.

The director sighed once more, this time unhappily. With his life firmly in the grip of developments he had no control over, this was one headache too many. He did not want to reason with this woman. Not that he would have been able to anyway. She was a world removed from him. He found these raw displays of emotion unpleasant and unnerving. He had never been comfortable with semi-literate sorts with their overt appeals to gods, their faith in rituals and exaggerated emotions. Half his headaches were caused by faculty meeting these precise criteria. And now, here was this woman appealing to him, blaming him, seeking succour of some sort from him.

'Madam, I'm not aware of any such thing.'

A fresh bout of hysterics greeted this.

'What will happen to me? My life is at an end. What have I done in my past life to deserve this? What will people say? What will they think? How can I face my neighbours after this? If you can't help me I must jump off the roof. What option do I have?'

'You could consult a lawyer. You could pray at a temple. You could go on a pilgrimage to Kedarnath. You could take an auto or bus and go home. You could believe me when I tell you that it is highly unlikely that your husband and Professor Thilakavathi are having an affair. You could believe me when I tell you that trespassers on the roof of this building will be prosecuted. You have plenty of options, madam.' Best to be literal about the whole thing, he thought. Avoid all those otherworldly excursions.

'But I saw them on his scooter.'

'And how many times did you see them on his scooter?'

'Only once. But that doesn't matter. You are supporting him. All you men support only men. Before jumping off the roof I shall tell the whole world that you were supporting that man.'

Visions of being chased around the campus by a rural mob intent on avenging Swapnasundari Sambandham's failed attempts at defying gravity danced before him.

'No, no. Please don't do that!'

'That Nilakantan master said to ask director…'

'Professor Nilakantan told you about this?'

It was clear she hadn't meant to mention his name. Reluctantly, her eyes avoiding his, she nodded.

'I shall ask my secretary to call Professor Nilakantan here.'

'No, no. Don't talk to him. Please don't call him!'

'Perhaps I should call professors Thilakavathi and Sambandham too. I could call the police as well.'

He watched with relief as she hurriedly gathered her things and scuttled out of the room. There was a brief moment of cheer at authority and wisdom exerted effectively before the weight of his situation brought him back to grim reality.

Decision-making in a Chaotic World

The joint chancellor's opening remarks were brief:

'Action. Chancellor always says that actions are better than words. So action is the theme and the reason for this meeting.'

APA 8 aka Arogyasami took over. Hard work and some minor organizational successes meant progress from a lowly APA 12 to his current status. Like his boss, he was ambitious. Real status meant APA 4 or better, and becoming PA itself was not complete wishful thinking. The PA was not to know any of this, of course. Arogyasami had been given responsibility for this event in Kovai. Normally, this would be seen as an exile to the furthest reaches of Dr Rakshasan's universe. Thootukudi or Srivilliputur would be worse, of course, implying a demotion from APA 8. But this was different. Dr A. Rakshasan, BA, BL, D.Litt., MP, was to grace this event, and the possibility of being noticed by the great man, the PA's boss himself, occupied centre stage in his thoughts and dreams. This was opportunity. Done right, APA 3, or even 2, was a distinct possibility. He cleared his throat and began to speak in Tamil.

The director understood soon enough that this functional equivalent of Jagan was calling the shots and that he, along with several other Sundarambal satraps, had to take down notes and orders.

'Chairman's followers' transportation facilities. Update please.'

The boss of the Sundarambal Transport Company responded. 'Five hundred and fifty seven buses already arranged. Another 125 on standby. Biryani packages all arranged. Parking arrangements are to be intimated. Also, one small matter requiring clarification.'

'Yes?'

'Please clarify which account head for expenses: diesel, biryani, brandy, beer, driver expenses, etc.'

'All expenses to be debited to Sundarambal Institute of Management.'

It took a long moment or two for this to register with the director, preoccupied as he was with making sure his papers were in order. The institute's P&L was his responsibility and here he was, casually blindsided by a runaway gravy-train of expenses.

'I really must register my strong protest,' he yelped.

APA 8 stared at him beadily. 'I...we...don't understand English.'

The director repeated himself in words that lost their force and emphasis in the course of their painful translation into Tamil. His way with words, something he took pride in as a useful way of keeping the illiterates at bay, could no longer be used as a rapier in the cut and thrust of debate. He sat defenceless before the heavily oiled, perfumed and mustachioed Sundarambal functionaries, aware that he stood out in every possible way.

APA 8 didn't blink. 'Invitation to Dr A. Rakshasan, BA, BL, D.Litt., MP, has come from you. As per rules, cost is to be borne by you.'

It occurred to the director that he hadn't, as a matter of fact, invited the chancellor for anything. Also, he hadn't yet found out who was responsible for this ridiculous situation. Hell, AICTE approval or no AICTE approval, he needed to up Agarwal's target. Ps, and more to the point, Ls, hung in the balance.

'Dr A. Rakshasan's three wives are also coming to witness ceremony. Suite rooms in hotels to be arranged. Separate hotels for each. Transportation arrangements to venue to be arranged. Senior wife to reach venue first and garland Dr A. Rakshasan who will already be seated at venue. She is to be seated to his left. Junior wife to reach second and garland Dr A. Rakshasan and senior wife before being seated to his right. Young wife to reach only after junior wife is seated. To garland Dr A. Rakshasan, senior wife and junior wife in correct sequence and be seated on a stool in front of Dr A. Rakshasan. Stool height such that Dr A. Rakshasan's face is visible to all supporters. AC car to be provided to all family dignitaries.' APA 8 looked pointedly at the director. 'Arrangements to be made by Sundarambal Institute of Management. Expenses debited to same. Any questions?'

'Me?' queried the director, more to himself than anything else.

APA 8 was not countenancing any question, rhetorical or otherwise.

'Yes, of course. Kindly update by tomorrow without fail. Chief guest update please?'

The chancellor was a member of the ruling party in the state and the director had decided to try the chief minister first. Getting access to someone in the CM's entourage hadn't been easy, getting a commitment even less so. He had finally received word, unofficially, that the chief minister had been upset that he wasn't the recipient of the honorary doctorate and that there was no way he would consider attending a function honouring a flunky like Rakshasan. Besides, if he started gracing functions like this, there would be no end to it. Officially, his office did not deign to reply.

An assistant to an officer at the PMO had sent a regulation letter regretting the prime minister's inability to attend, along with his best wishes. Knowing that the chancellor and his acolytes were unlikely to accept these regrets with equanimity, he had put out the word that he was short – desperately short – a VIP to grace a function. Coimbatore in May lacked the charm of spring in London or Paris and the regrets piled up like snowdrifts in winter. There was one, just one, hint at a possible yes and this he clung to like a drowning man would his rope.

'Poojya Guruji, Sri Sri Sri Rambhakta Swami of Delhi, is likely to visit Kovai around that time. With the chairman's permission I would like to invite him.'

Silence. The joint chancellor and APA 8 stared coldly at him. His fellow Sundarambal chieftains found interesting ways to avoid eye contact. Poojya Guruji, for the uninitiated, ticked all the wrong boxes from the perspective of a blue-blooded Tamil politician. He was a Brahmin, a North Indian and a Hindi speaker. Having him grace the function would be like Rama blessing Ravana's nuptials, only worse.

The director stared back defiantly. He had tried his best, but there were just no takers. If *this* was going to be the reason for his sacking, well, there were worse things in life.

'Why him?' the joint chancellor finally spoke.

'He is on the prime minister's advisory committee on management education. He is also one of the PM's closest advisors. The PM sends his best wishes but regrets that he is unable to come.'

'PM sent best wishes?' APA 8 was quick on the draw.

'That was what his office said…'

'This is very important news. The prime minister himself is wishing our beloved and great Dr A. Rakshasan, BA, BL, D.Litt., MP. Tomorrow itself this has to be in the paper, this news of PM felicitating our beloved leader.' APA 8 looked around, trying to decide which of the assembled satraps should be entrusted with this responsibility. The boss-man of Sundarambal TV got the nod. The director sent up a silent prayer of thanks.

Back to Poojya Guruji. The pros and cons were finely balanced: having someone utterly inimical to Tamil political culture (read: Rakshasan's political future) versus not having a chief guest at all. Appearances were key and demonstrating that you could get 50,000 'followers' to drop whatever they were doing and trek down to Kovai fuelled only by biryani and brandy was one part of this. Demonstrating to the 50,000 that someone even more important than their leader was willing to make the same trek to praise him was the complementary bit. One without the other was like a politician without his veshti.

APA 8 knew better than to ask if the CM had been invited. The satraps were a fickle lot, he knew, ready to throw in their lot with a political rival at the slightest hint that their leader was out of favour.

'I shall discuss with Leader and revert,' he said finally.

They moved on with the agenda. The design of the welcome arch, the plastering of posters all over town, the size and shape of the pandal and the arrangements for broadcasting the leader's words of wisdom were all discussed. The director had little to say or do in all of this other than note the alarming accumulation of expenses, all debited to his account.

One issue cropped up, which did call for his expert opinion. Whether, as the recipient of a second honorary doctorate, Leader should henceforth be referred to as Dr Dr Rakshasan.

The director promised to constitute a faculty committee to look into the matter and even the joint chancellor saw the wisdom of referring this question to a committee.

Bargaining sessions were times Agarwal lived for: there was something deeply satisfying about the to-ing and fro-ing, the sharing of tea and snacks, the digging deep into his mental resources for the appropriate responses and the exaggerated reactions and emotions.

The director had never been his favourite negotiating adversary. For one thing, he gave in too easily. And, there were too many awkward silences. Their many differences were never more evident than those odd times when he was called in for one of *those* discussions. Worst, tea and snacks were never on offer. This lack of the obligatory ice-breaking cup of chai was something he never could get used to.

Some of this, he sensed, came from the awkward circumstances of his hiring – circumstances that only he and the director were privy to. He was there to recruit students. The fig-leaf of teaching notwithstanding, he was there *only* to recruit students. He was there to persuade residents of the broad Gangetic plains that their managerial careers would be best served by the long trek past the Vindhyas and Satpuras, through the red soil and granitic eruptions of the Deccan, down the rolling plains of western Tamil Nadu and into the hallowed Sundarambal portals. That his real work took place during the term breaks, and that there were substantial performance bonuses attached to his efforts, were things he and the director kept to themselves. This shared secret knowledge meant awkwardness, short meetings, and relief when business had been concluded.

This time, though, despite an outcome he had

no quarrel with, Agarwal found himself even more dissatisfied than usual. The meeting was over even before he had curled into a comfortable slouch.

'Professor Agarwal, more students. I want more students. Quick. Signed up and fees paid.'

'But...' he began settling himself into the familiar cadences of negotiation.

'Your terms. This needs to be done quick.'

'One lakh per...' he began cautiously.

'Of course. Done.' The director reached across the table and a stunned Agarwal limply shook his hand. 'That's all. Thank you. And do keep me updated when you round up...er, sign up, some students. This is urgent, very urgent. So, quick.'

Shit! Now that he was done with the director, he knew he had been had. Not cheated, exactly, but he could have, should have, held out for more. He should have guessed from the director's face. The man looked desperate. But...and now the doubts grew. Students were never easy to persuade. Convincing them to join the institute urgently... Well, where were they going to come from? The money was all very nice but these students needed to believe that the money they were putting into the chancellor's pocket meant an education and improved career prospects.

'This idli–dosa issue is a major problem. They come here from Meerut, Bulandshahr, Rohtak, all those kind of places, having dal, sabji, roti, paranthas and jalebis for breakfast, samosa and kachoris for tea, and here they are complaining. They complain about many things but first and foremost they complain about not having dal sabji. What difficulties!' Agarwal sighed as he contemplated the difficulties.

'Studies vudies okay, na?' There weren't too many North Indians in Coimbatore and only a few of them were banias, but these lost souls had found each other and met to discuss business over cups of masala chai, kachoris and chat. Gupta ran a coaching centre for MBA aspirants. The two frequently exchanged gossip and tips and had a shared interest in growing the ranks of business students.

'Haan, that is okay. Syllabus villabus all same whether here or Rohtak. Only, this Madrasi accent is causing some problems. Still, they get a free laptop. Internet keeps them occupied, so they are noticing the accent less. One issue with the free laptops, though. Some students are asking for PowerPoint, not lectures. I ask you Guptaji, what is the point of this PowerPoint? After all, my father and his father all studied and wrote exams without the benefit of this PowerPoint. Myself and yourself, if I am not greatly mistaken, also did college without PowerPoint. Even Sardar Patel and Swami Vivekananda and many others as well.'

'Hundred per cent agreed. These days students are spoilt. Always asking for more and more. You know that "dil maange more" advertisement? Bad idea I tell you. Putting wrong ideas into young heads.'

'And that is exactly my problem now.'

'The young heads have wrong ideas?'

'No, no. The director says "yeh dil maange more". More students, even more students. Two times now he has called me. Always the same thing: more students. It is April now, students are already choosing where to study and he says he wants more students quickly. Guptaji, do you have any ideas?'

Gupta scratched his head. 'Agarwalji, before CAT exam, no problem. Students are asking where to apply and I can give good advice. Sundarambal Institute will give free laptop, canteen serving good food, therefore good place to apply. Also excellent faculty like your good self, of course. But now? Next year's CAT preparation starts only in July. I have no students now. What can I do?'

'*Haan*, this problem is there. What choice do I have now? Running around Haryana and UP in summer is terrible but I have no choice in this matter. And these students, so many choices they are having these days. I am asking you, Guptaji, is it right for a faculty like myself to be begging students? They have no respect for elders, for teachers. This Teachers' Day that they are celebrating, I am always asking my fellow faculty members, what are they celebrating? Have we anything to celebrate? Students today are very spoilt. In the old days did we complain when we got tinda lauki in canteen? Did we say, aloo gobi only?'

Gupta looked sheepish. 'Actually, Agarwalji, one year we burned down the canteen in protest. One full week they served only tinda lauki. Next week we burned down the canteen.'

'Yes, but not every year, no?'

'What are you saying? Of course, only once when I was there.'

'But today, every student I am talking to is saying, you are asking me to study in Madras, only idli-dosa available there. Questions about college? No. Questions about syllabus? No. Questions about jobs and suchlike? No. Food, and only food. This is the state of matters today. Very difficult for me. And after coming here, the same story. Complaints about sambar and rasam only. Questions about management subjects? Nothing.'

Gupta nodded sympathetically. 'Maybe we can go into business? Start a mess serving chapati and dal and aloo-gobi and rajma. All those students you are getting here, there will be sufficient demand. This coaching business, for six months there is no business. Mess business will be better business, I feel.'

'Not to forget kachoris and masala chai. That canteen is only serving coffee and dip chai. No masala chai, can you believe? Excellent idea, Guptaji, but first I need to solve this students problem. To run a successful mess you need students. Many students. In fact, many North Indian students. Otherwise who will be appreciating your chapati and dal and aloo gobi? Guptaji, any suggestions you have in this regard will be most appreciated.'

'Professorji, you are a true management *ka ustad*. What insights you are giving! No customer, no business. Here I am thinking about business opportunities. There you are reminding me that without customers there can be no business. Your students are lucky to have such a professor.'

Professorji wasn't entirely sure that his leg wasn't being pulled. But in their long acquaintance, he had never seen Gupta take life less seriously than his aloo gobi and *that* was a very serious business, testified to by Mrs Gupta's indentured servitude in the kitchen. This was praise, then, high praise even, and he shrugged modestly. 'These students are keeping us faculty on our toes. No time for chai even. They ask top-class questions in class. They want to know about new developments in management. Guptaji, you know that in the old days I used to teach Industrial Relations. These days I teach Human Capital Management. *Ek dum* up-to-date.'

'What a privilege it is to be your friend, Agarwalji! But if these students are having no time for chai shai, how will we sell aloo gobi?'

'Food for stomach is not taking back seat to food for mind. You see, a healthy mind requires a healthy body. And a healthy body requires aloo gobi.'

'Wah! Kya logic!'

'But we need many healthy bodies. Back to the old problem. From where do we get bodies?'

'Agarwalji, one idea is coming into my mind.'

'Yes?'

'You see, some other institutes here are having interviews for their MBA courses. Three–four institutes, maybe more, and students will be coming here from many places.'

'Many students?'

'Oh yes. MBA degree has become very popular. So we can persuade students that Sundarambal is an option, maybe with laptop and canteen and faculties like your good self in addition.'

'Hmm.'

'Of course, we will have to do some marketing sharketing.'

'The Sundarambal laptop advantage.'

'*Wah*!'

'Rose is for beauty, and Sundarambal is for study.'

'Professorji, you are a poet in addition to being a guru!'

'Sundarambal to learn, then you get job to earn.'

'*Ustad!*'

'Heh, heh, sometimes these thoughts come to my head. But your idea is something. I shall devote some time to it. Deep thinking on the subject is needed.'

The presence of the computer on his desk notwithstanding, old-fashioned paper and a Parker bequeathed to him by his father were the director's stock-in-trade. That pen, to him, was a symbol of the decay and loss of values that had permeated life and society. A Parker in those days meant something. A rejection of cheap Japanese goods. An appreciation of class rather than ostentation. Money well spent rather than being frittered away. The other day he had gone to a stationer's and had been appalled to find Parkers being sold in cheap plastic bubble wrap for Rs 125.

Parkers! The faculty he had these days were like those 125-rupee Parkers. A travesty. Good for absolutely nothing other than noise and hot air.

He looked at the well-worn AICTE missive and sighed heavily. No point expecting any sort of cooperation from that lot, he'd have to take care of the bloody lacunae himself. He ticked off item 6. Thirteen dustbins had been purchased and he hoped to God no one would complain that this had been done without a dustbin purchasing committee.

Item 7. The offending men's urinal had been removed and had cracked in the process. One for the L column. The wall behind the erstwhile urinal had not received its fair share of paint and this, in turn, had been rectified to forestall any further AICTE mischief. More L.

The course titles had all been changed. He had also had Jagan collect sworn affidavits from a bunch of students stating that this change had not led to any confusion, that they were clear about the managerial path laid out for them by Sundarambal. No harm in taking additional precautions – abundant caution was the technical term for this sort of servile arse-covering.

Item 2. If only everything was as simple as this. Sundarambal was 14 hours short of the requisite 1440 hours of education. One per cent. One, and only one per cent for heaven's sake. The one per cent that perhaps made all the difference between a competent manager and an incompetent sociopath. The one per cent that AICTE, ever vigilant, had identified as the crucial ingredient which transformed a frothy, simmering broth into one of the leaders who would take the country into a better, managerially competent, tomorrow. The hell with it. They wanted one per cent, he'd give them that and more. An additional hour pencilled in for each of the courses. There. Three whole per cent, give or take a bit. Sundarambal would now provide the vanguard of the new managerial cadre. All the rest, silly them, trailing behind with their pathetic one per cents, providing mere foot-soldiers to the new managerial movement. Courtesy the ever-vigilant AICTE, of course.

He shook himself free of his stream of consciousness reverie as he contemplated Item 9. The nub of the matter. The rats. The same rats that had Sambandham and his idiot colleagues in an incoherent, noisy, babble, the same rats which had reduced him to an inglorious clerical scribe, a humble servant begging to remain, yours completely insincerely. The local office of AICTE had a list (certified) of rat catchers. It had taken them two days to find it: they knew that no paper ever left a government office, and, secure in this knowledge, they exercised due diligence before finally unearthing it.

Jagan had been entrusted with the task of obtaining the services of a rat catcher. It turned out that none of the three certified rat catchers in the district were still in the business. They now ran coaching classes for MBA entrance tests and wanted no reminder of their past. A brief spark of hope ran through the director when he heard this news. But no. Their students were all placed. The next year? Sundarambal was not on their preferred list, though this could be rectified for a fee, said fee reflecting the presence of the rats in the canteen. The director said he would get back to them. Not that he planned to. He had entrusted his future to Agarwal. Better the known devil than some semiliterate rat catchers. Not to mention the judgement shown by students who had entrusted their futures to these worthies.

This meant that the rats (two in numbers) continued, unimpeded, to impede the learning process at Sundarambal. Managerial careers continued to hang in the balance.

There was the Rat Kill option, of course. He had no doubt that any product from the Rakshasan stable would guarantee wholesale elimination of life. It was the humane detachment of life from its moorings that was in question. Rat Kill's impact on the delicate sensibilities of the students was also in question. Not in question was AICTE's earnest concern for the students' mental well-being. It was a vexing dilemma, one to which great management thinkers had provided no answers.

The hell with it, he finally decided. Rat Kill it would be. He couldn't help it if AICTE didn't/couldn't update its empowered panel of humane rat eliminators.

Leadership

Dr A. Rakshasan, BA, BL, D.Litt., MP, was an important man, the master of his universe. Like many public figures, his origins were obscure, his path to wealth and prominence the subject of myth rather than fact. It was said that he had started out as a driver. With an ego and ambition quite at variance with his modest status, he had doggedly made his way up the economic and social ladder, keeping his ultimate goals in mind while using what means came to hand.

Now, with three wives, numerous villas, a seat in Parliament, an honorary doctorate and a level of social acceptance that even he found acceptable, he lorded over a business empire that encompassed education, aviation, transport, liquor, mining and broadcast television. He was an important man, a busy man, a man whose whereabouts at any given point in time were a mystery even to those most near and dear to him.

Late mornings, that odd interval when thoughts of the next meal were a distant abdominal murmur, when her daughters, petulant and difficult, had been packed off to their school and when the distant, filtered sounds of the street were all that disturbed the quiet of her room, were when her thoughts ran back in time.

She had been a romantic, a talcum powder, jasmine flower, film song sort of romantic. A tree that she could hug and run around, a hillside where she could elude the grasp of a reaching lover, flowers touching romantically in the sunlight: the landscape of her dreams was a simple one.

She had simpered when he smiled at her, blushed furiously when he spoke to her, and then tried to imitate those ladies who knew how to feign disinterest even while letting the man of their dreams know that they were interested. He looked like a film star, his thick hair oiled and swept back in shiny waves, wearing clothes that were an iridescent cascade down carefully nonchalant flanks, and speaking words that worked magic on her innocent, receptive mind.

Words failed her when he spoke to her, her giggles didn't, and she spent her nights alternating between an ecstasy of dreams and a rank fear that he would tire of her.

'My jasmine,' he said.

She giggled coquettishly. 'You mustn't say such things.'

'You are my beautiful jasmine. My name for you will be Jasmine.'

'You are very wicked.' This was said as she moved languorously around an imaginary tree. He followed her around with a lecherous grin. She looked coy. He grabbed at her. She allowed him a handhold and feigned helpless distress.

One morning he took her to a temple. It was an auspicious temple for marriage, he told her, and the day and the hour were auspicious as well. The stars would never again be aligned in their favour, something the well-bribed priest was happy to confirm. The circumstances were too much for her; like the heroines she admired she succumbed to the favourable omens and holy surroundings and married him.

That afternoon they became man and wife at a lodge close to the temple.

That evening, the reality of her situation hit her. Between sunrise and sunset she had become a married woman not just in the eyes of God but at the hands of this rake. He would have preferred to have left her parents in the dark. Her woman's intuition told her that in her case, an early disclosure would be infinitely preferable and far less embarrassing than a later one. The threat of a police complaint ensured that he saw things in a similar light. Those were days when the threat of a police complaint meant something to him.

It was bad enough news for her parents to hear that this perfumed, slick character with the airs and attitude of a B-grade film star was now their son-in-law. Both broke down when they heard that their daughter's surname was now Rakshasan.

The years went by and the romantic ruffian she had married became Dr Rakshasan, Leader. He was still a ruffian but the romance had left her life. As a matter of fact *he* had left her life as well.

Not that he left her in need of anything. She lived with the girls in a centrally air-conditioned house provided by him. The girls wanted fine clothes and jewellery and got it. He paid for them to go to a school with air-conditioned classrooms. He paid for the servants who ensured that she would become fat, lazy and addicted to family melodramas on TV. But there was no denying the fact that she was now a peripheral presence in his scheme of things.

She had not minded his absences at first. He was her man, but he needed to make his way in life and who was she to stand in his way? His life, she learnt once the two girls had bound her even more tightly to him, included an earlier wife, sons and much else besides. Becoming fat, lazy and addicted to family melodramas was her way of coping with post-traumatic stress disorder.

'My Jasmine darling!'

She dropped the phone in her confusion, then scurried to retrieve it before he changed his mind and hung up. She had marked the third anniversary of his last telephone call a few weeks earlier.

'My master! My leader! Father of my daughters! It is you! Is this a dream?'

'Good news I am having and your presence I am needing.'

'Yes, of course, yes. Your every wish I am...'

'P.K. will be calling you about details.'

'I am so happy! What is this good news? We shall all be sharing this good news...'

The flat hum of a hung-up phone. The tedium of the morning. The last exhalation of expectations.

'Madam, kindly take notes.'

She scrambled to obey. She still remembered P.K. as a thin flunky in vests and shorts. Like the rest of the Leader's circle, he was now fat and obnoxious. And, like the Leader, he didn't allow her to interrupt.

'Ceremony in Kovai concerning doctoral degree of Leader. Second May. Transportation and suite room in hotel to be provided. Ceremony to proceed as follows. Senior madam, junior madam – namely yourself – and young madam to be seated on stage. Senior madam to be seated on left of throne, yourself on right of throne, young madam on stool in front of Leader. When Leader comes, young madam to touch your feet, you and young madam to touch senior madam's feet, then all madams to prostrate before Leader seeking blessings. On signal, resume seating position. Rehearsal to take place first May. Dress rehearsal second May.'

P.K.'s staccato burst abruptly ceased, leaving only the hum of the phone to accompany her in her solitude. She went over her hastily scribbled notes. And realized that she was now a mere filler between senior madam and young madam.

Dr Rakshasan was a firm believer in ritual. Elaborate rituals marked his interactions with the Almighty. Equally elaborate rituals marked his interactions with his fellow human beings. Public functions were choreographed to the last detail. He had an immense sense of self and wanted his followers to see him for the important, highly respected man that he was. His image required it, his ego demanded it. P.K. and his flunkies were in charge of ensuring it.

P.K. himself had assumed charge as choreographer-in-chief: the Sundarambal function had been deemed too important to be left to an APA 8. APAs lacked the experience and imagination needed to ensure that followers didn't go home wishing that they had watched a Rajinikanth movie instead. With 50,000 followers expected, the choreography needed to be special.

'The usual procedure is for the conferee to bow to the person conferring the degree before accepting the scroll.' The director was trying to explain the normal procedure for the conferral of honorary doctorates.

'No. Leader only bows to *his* leader and to God. This chief guest is not even a leader. Out of the question.'

'What would you suggest, then?'

'Chief guest bows to Leader.'

'Chief guest can also touch Leader's feet.' APA 8 wasn't about to be left out of these important deliberations.

'Yes, chief guest can bow to Leader and then touch his feet. Kindly keep minutes.'

It took the director a moment to understand that the secretarial functions had been assigned to him. A feeling of deep loathing, made worse by the knowledge that he could do nothing about it, had taken hold of him. He attended to his secretarial duties with a frown.

'Just touching or full prostrating?' APA 8 was not done.

'Excuse me, but shouldn't someone check with the chief guest whether this is acceptable to him?' The director felt constrained to inject a note of reality into the proceedings.

'Chief guest doesn't want to touch feet and prostrate before our Leader?' P.K. and APA 8 couldn't believe what they were hearing.

'Without checking with him, how would I know?'

'Everyone wants to touch feet and prostrate before our Leader. The entire state of Tamil Nadu, people from US, Singapore and South America even, all of them want to touch our Leader's feet and prostrate before him. Kindly inform this to the chief guest.'

'The chief guest is the PM's representative. I cannot ask him. I mean, he is the chief guest, we invited him, we cannot very well ask him to prostrate before the chancellor.'

'Leader.'

'Yes, yes, our Leader who is also our respected and beloved chancellor.'

P.K. shot the director a sharp look. This man was creating unnecessary trouble.

'If he doesn't respect our Leader, why have you made him chief guest? Since you made him chief guest, kindly inform him that everyone wants to prostrate themselves before Leader. Next?'

Uncertain silence.

'Thiru director, I am asking, after touching feet and prostrating what is the next item in the ceremony?'

'Oh. Ah. Well, the chief guest hands over the scroll. The chancellor...Leader...thanks him and walks back to his seat.'

'That is all?'

'Well, generally, yes.'

P.K. shook his head.

'That is not enough. This is a big, very important, function. More ceremony is needed, more... functioning...is needed. And why no speeches? Big function for Leader and no speeches? Why?'

'What would you suggest?'

'Thiru director, you have requested Leader for this function. Suggesting is your job.'

'We can certainly include speeches if that's what Leader wants.'

'Leader doesn't want. Followers of Leader want. Me and you want. You also want, don't you?'

'Yes, of course. There is nothing I want more than a long speech by the Leader. I get the point. By popular request, a speech by the Leader after he is conferred his degree.'

'Just handing over degree and speech? Not enough. This is a big...'

'Yes, yes, I can see where your queries are going. How about the chief guest tapping the leader on the shoulder with a sword, like the queen does with her knights.' Might as well have some fun, he thought, but felt it prudent to leave out the bit about the knights-to-be kneeling before the queen.

'Queen? What queen?'

'The British queen. Queen Elizabeth.'

'Diana's mother-in-law?'

'That's the one.'

'Taps shoulder with sword at important ceremonies?'

'In the Buckingham Palace, her London palace.'

'Oh. Interesting idea. Leader might appreciate this. Followers will greatly appreciate it.' Silence all around while P.K. gave it some thought. 'But there is one issue.'

'Yes?'

'You see, swords are very thin. Followers in the back may not be able to follow the action.'

'We plan to have TVs installed throughout the pandals.'

'But even with TV, sword profile is not satisfactory. Why not a mace?'

'Mace?'

'Yes, yes, like the one Bhima is using in Mahabharata. Very visible for all the followers.'

'P.K. sir, begging your pardon but I most humbly foresee one problem.'

'Yes, Arogyasami?'

'Mace is very heavy, and if it slips...'

'Cardboard mace we will have, painted gold in colour. Thiru director, you shall arrange for this too. Kindly examine maces used by Sivaji Ganesan in various films and make design in accordance. Also *ponnadai*. Silk with gold jari work. Purchase from Sundarambal Sari Stores. Good! Now I have decided. Ceremony shall be as follows. Chief guest bows and prostrates before Leader. Touches feet. Then puts *ponnadai* around Leader, which Leader humbly accepts. Then chief guest takes mace and taps on shoulder like British Queen. Then confers degree. Then Leader accepts request to give speech. Any questions?'

Poojya Guruji looked his usual calm self. Those who knew him well, though, could tell that he was very upset.

'My recollection is that *they* approached *us*. I am not mistaken, am I?' Spoken quietly, in a matter-of-fact way. Those who didn't know him would have missed the hint of something different in the voice. The messenger did, and knew that he was the bearer of ill tidings.

He looked at his feet and tried to moisten his dry lips. 'Poojya Guruji, these people, they are not like us. They are very difficult to deal with. There were six of them standing around me.'

'Haven't I taught you to distance yourself from the here and now? Haven't I taught you to achieve that clarity of thought that comes from a deliberate pushing aside of worldly concerns? Haven't I taught you that decisions are best made when the mind is free of temporal stresses?'

'They had sickles with them, Poojya Guruji.'

'What?'

'Sickles. Those sharp-edged, curved, agricultural implements. The edges were sharp, I can confirm from personal experience.'

'They threatened you?'

'It was very difficult to keep the mind free of temporal stress under the circumstances. I know

I've let you down, Poojya Guruji, but I have to plead extenuating circumstances.'

Poojya Guruji's expression didn't change but his concern was evident.

'In the circumstances, perhaps it is best that we respectfully decline the invitation. With regret and pleading extenuating circumstances, of course. Are we agreed on this?'

'Poojya Guruji?'

'Yes?'

'They anticipated this reaction. In the course of our meeting, they made it clear that there would be consequences to such a course of action.'

'Meaning? If we don't go there, what can they do to us here? This is Delhi, *our* territory.'

'They have somehow got wind of the retreat we are putting up.'

'And?'

'This Rakshasan evidently has a herd of pet elephants that they turn loose when arguments don't go their way.'

'I'm not sure I like the sound of this. What kind of people are these, anyway?'

'They are people who mean what they say. That herbal garden which was coming up so nicely at your retreat was trampled over. Completely destroyed. Those pet elephants. They forced me to watch. They mean business and this was meant as a token of their intent.'

Poojya Guruji's figure slumped in despair.

The Regulatory Perspective

An excerpt from the diary of Mr Santosh Hota, IAS, deputy secretary, Ministry of Human Resource Development:

These things are a huge ego boost and I can see why these AICTE panel chappies are quite happy fooling around on these inspection tours. Bangalore (sorry, Bengaluru, never know when someone might take offence, but doesn't it say / mean something when that pesky spell-checker squiggles red for Bengaluru and not for Bangalore?) yesterday, but the Bangalore we saw occupies that odd penumbra between the IT glass-and-concrete, manicured-lawn, high-intellect Bangalore and those shady, sullen neighbourhoods where old Bangalore grumbles about what is and the peaceful, traffic-and-crowd-free days of an era gone by.

Obsequious. The way we do it, the word itself conveys insincerity, an excess of oil and false flattery and a subtext of favours toted up and exchanged.

There were four of us and two Mercedes cars at our disposal. Two were 'academic experts', small-time people from small-time colleges sitting in judgement over their peers, the third an AICTE bureaucrat. We met over dinner the previous day. No one seemed surprised at the quality of the accommodation and transportation on offer. There was a distinct pause in the chit-chat and something else – caution? awe? respect? – when they heard who I was. I suppose there *is* something to be learnt from these types. I tried to draw them out. No luck. Authority is always seen as authority: they turned down the second round of drinks with poorly concealed regret and called it an early night. Not that I minded. Obsequiousness was starting to seep out around the edges and this lot had yet to figure out how to do it properly.

The girls with the garlands and *tilak* were a nice touch, two of them for each of us, taking us on what I assumed was a carefully choreographed tour of the facilities. No boys in sight and I checked my file to confirm that this *was* a co-ed institute. So where are all the boys, I wanted to know, and they blushed and giggled so prettily that I hadn't the heart to probe further. Troublemakers all, clearly, and best kept away from inspectors and itinerant IAS officers. Library, auditorium – why does everyone insist on showing off their auditorium? – classrooms, computer lab.

I slipped into a class in progress. They were expecting me and rose as though ordered by a drill sergeant. Boys in blazers on one side, girls in saris on the other. The instructor kept bowing and smiling until I sat and nodded. This class was on logistics, he told me, and did I have any questions for his students? Why not,

I thought to myself, a break from this choreographed tedium. The question was an anodyne one, whether the new Chinese-built port in southern Sri Lanka would have an impact on our own southern ports. The girls smiled prettily, the boys gaped blankly, the instructor looked embarrassed and silence hung in the air. Broken, finally, by an apologetic instructor. My question, evidently, was not covered in the syllabus. I was requested to kindly excuse. Oh, well. I asked him to continue his class which he did in a stilted voice, the students dutifully jotting down notes until I got up to leave and the drill-sergeant routine was repeated for my benefit. I'm sure they were as relieved at my departure as I was.

The others were done with their tour as well and we got down to the business end of our visit. My presence had upset some equilibrium and the director kept looking nervously at me. The academic experts had a checklist, various documents were produced and questions were asked. I had the feeling this was all for my benefit, that this meeting would have gone differently in my absence. This fussing with minutiae, this ticking of boxes, bored me and the urge to set the cat among the pigeons was overwhelming. What did he, the director, think of Mintzberg's critique of traditional management education? Another embarrassed silence and I couldn't help revelling in his discomfiture.

Time, an awkward, stilted fifteen minutes or so, to meet the faculty who were unanimous in their praise of the freedom and facilities afforded them by the institute's management. I gave Mintzberg a pass and spent my time staring at the female faculty. Age and experience had done little to help them, and the relief when we left for lunch was mutual.

A five-star lunch followed by an afternoon inspection which went along familiar lines. *This* director felt that Mintzberg was not suitable for Indian conditions. He didn't seem surprised at my question: the grapevine clearly works during lunch breaks. No surprise then that news of the Chinese–Sri Lankan port had also spread, the students having been told in between drill-sergeant routines that this was an exemplar of that contentious management phenomenon: globalization.

I needed to limit the time spent in the company of the academic experts – too much of that and I'd end up an academic expert myself. So I'm meeting up with some batchmates: some drinks, dinner and meaningful conversation for a change.

Another day of this and then off to Coimbatore. Sinha is joining me there. If *this* is Bangalore, the city that keeps Obama awake at night, what's in store for us in Coimbatore?

Understanding your Customer II

Agarwal watched the crowds make their noisy way out of the station. The tea stall he was sitting in was inconspicuous, a hole-in-the-wall catering to travellers in a hurry. It afforded him a good view of all the comings and goings at the Coimbatore Station. The comings were what he kept a close eye on.

Gupta's intelligence had indicated that several batches of students were due that morning.

Some of the other management institutes in the area, also eager to broaden their catchment areas, had formed an informal consortium. They had coordinated their dates for the student interviews. Potential students, lured by the prospect of multiple shots at the MBA target for the price of a single train ticket, had marked out Coimbatore as a particularly promising destination. From Meerut and Rohtak, from Arrah, Chapra and Muzzafarpur, from Giridih, Jasidih, Dhanbad and Hazaribagh, they had made their way through the summer landscape, dreams of an MBA admission firmly in mind.

Sundarambal was not part of that consortium. There was a pecking order even in the lower reaches of the MBA hierarchy. Sundarambal was looked down upon even by this modest bunch: it had not been invited to join the consortium. Academic standards were cited as an excuse but concern about Dr Rakshasan's business ethics and doubts about whether his institutes could be relied on to keep their informal word were the real reason for their pariah status.

Agarwal's expense account had allowed him some room for planning and manoeuvre. Representatives of other institutes had been stationed with placards on the platforms. But when the trains rolled in, they were all absent – one had stepped away for refreshments, another to answer nature's call, a third to check out the news stand, a fourth to indulge his train-spotting hobby. Agarwal had a trader's instinct for a deal, but had taken no chances. Two-timers were a dime a dozen and he needed to be absolutely sure that no one reneged on their deal. Lurking in the shadows were toughs, there to point out facts and consequences to waverers, to ensure that Agarwal's carefully laid plans hatched correctly. These then took their places, complete with placards and helpful directions.

As the trains rolled in, the students were corralled by the placard-waving toughs and herded into waiting buses whose signs had been altered for the occasion. They chattered away, happy that their long journeys were done with, anticipating interviews in their institutions of choice. They took in the street scenes, the huge placards with cut-outs of strange politicians and film stars, the signs in a script no one understood, the sights and sounds of a world they had never before seen.

Agarwal knew that the students needed to be securely housed and had given the matter much thought. The students needed to be hidden from the competition. They were not to be allowed to change their minds. They needed to be kept safe until Sundarambal was ready to receive them. He got word about a retreat, owned by some yoga guru, in the foothills well away from the city. Accommodation was arranged by bribing the security and frightening them into silence by invoking the name of Dr Rakshasan.

The bustle and din of the city were soon left behind. The buses headed towards Mettupalayam and the foothills of the Nilgiris. The students were pleased. They had heard that the region they knew as Madras – that large swathe of southern India populated by Madrasis, Rajinikanth and A.R. Rehman – was hot and dry. Here was greenery, rolling hills and pleasant breezes. The buses turned off the main road and wound their way through fields and patches of forest. Large lumps of dried elephant droppings lay scattered around. An ornate, saffron-painted arch finally appeared and the buses drove past elaborate wrought-iron gates.

Back in the tea stall, Agarwal added up his numbers. Phase one of Operation Student had gone through without a hitch and he allowed himself a sigh of satisfaction. Now came the tough bit: getting those signatures on the dotted line and on the cheques.

He was into uncharted territory now and making it up as he went along. Time to put into play all those human relations tricks he had lectured about. Time to demonstrate that there was more to this old dog than reading from yellowing dog-eared textbooks.

There was plenty of beer, butter chicken, keema-naan, dal makhni and biryani for the students over the next two days. A lakh per student meant that Agarwal didn't have to skimp on the goodies to maintain his profit margins. He had erred on the side of plenty to ensure a happy, compliant bunch who hadn't a clue that they were involuntarily incarcerated.

It was a cheerful lot that were manhandled, or staggered, into the waiting buses when the time came for them to leave. Snatches of songs, good-natured bantering, shouts to unseen or distant comrades, drunken stumbling: there was an all-pervasive air of good cheer.

The minders were present, of course. Given Agarwal's efforts, they had little to do other than to keep the students pointed in approximately the right direction and ensuring that any nuisance was committed before they got into the buses. Like content sheep, the students flocked into the buses. Once filled, these made their way down the Nilgiri foothills, eventually joining the highway heading towards the Sundarambal campus. There were other buses headed the same way, something that the students, happy, noisy and content, did not notice.

Well-sluiced and fed students tend to leave a destructive trail in their wake and plenty of evidence of this was on offer by the time the students were done. They left behind a wrecked retreat. They had done a thorough job on anything the elephants had left intact. Broken windows, doors hanging off their hinges, fans with blades missing, mattresses with their stuffing missing, shattered ceramic in the bathrooms: all bore witness to youthful potential unleashed.

Poojya Guruji's plans for a retreat in the sylvan, silent foothills of the Nilgiris had taken yet another beating.

Managing Cultural Differences

Poojya Guruji did not like traffic jams.

In his discourses he often spoke of the flow of life and the necessity of living in sync with the divinely ordained flow that formed a backdrop to all lives. In the more congenial environs of Delhi, he had the means and influence to ensure that others adjusted to his flow. Progress – material, temporal and spatial – formed the pulse of his life. Prior to his arrival in Coimbatore there had been unwelcome reminders that he had to march to another drummer's beat. Now that he was here, though, there was no beat at all. His car was involuntarily stalled, surrounded by buses filled with noisy, excited Tamilians.

He wasn't sure if the loud shouts of *paapaan* were exuberant greetings or something worse. The acolyte seated in front had a grim look about him.

'What are they saying?'

'Poojya Guruji, I think they've noticed our saffron robes. *Paapaan* is a derogatory term for Brahmin.'

'Do people here always make so much noise? Are we safe?'

'I don't think they would actually *do* anything. They like to imitate local film stars but it's mostly bark rather than bite. But better we play safe and smile and wave at them.'

This Poojya Guruji did, his lack of enthusiasm concealed by the tinted windows. His wave provoked another round of whistles and cheers. He waved nervously again and was rewarded with cheers once more. One group got out from a bus and began dancing on the road. Their movements bore the influence of alcohol. They beat out a cheerful tattoo on Poojya Guruji's car to accompany their moves. This did nothing to further Poojya Guruji's sense of calm and general well-being. His features settled into a fixed look that his followers would have recognized.

'Machan!'

'Dai!'

The speaker rose unsteadily even as the bus he was riding on bounced and careened its way through and around potholes, cattle and assorted other obstacles. The person he was addressing was seated atop another bus moving in the same direction.

'Super prandhi, da!'

Liberally sluiced by pre- and post-prandial partaking of *prandhi* (a delectable grape derivative known elsewhere as brandy), the followers were in a happy daze. Politics was fun and Leader was a great man who knew how to give his followers a great time.

'*Paaru, da*!' He opened his fly and let loose. The movement of the bus combined with his random lurches meant that the stream jagged this way and that. Mixed cheers and protests greeted his efforts at target practice. The target, a large car with tinted windows, boxed in and with nowhere to go, somehow escaped unscathed.

'Idiot! What sort of aim is this? Missing a big car like that!'

'If Rajini was here, his piss would have become an arrow and correctly hit the car aerial!'

'What are you saying? It would have bounced off the car like a laser and drenched the villain!'

'*Muttal*! Watch where you are doing it!' The stream had claimed some collateral, non-villainous, damage.

An arm flung a bottle up from the bowels of the bus. Like much else, it missed its target, bouncing off the roof and onto the large car with tinted windows. The car swerved, to loud cheers from the onlookers. The car-as-target concept quickly caught on. Missiles of varied provenance were flung. Many missed, some did not. A few, finding no suitable object at hand, directed streams of paan at the car. Again, misses outnumbered the hits, but no one was keeping count amidst the general mirth.

The lurches of the bus combined with all the food and drink led to a few feeling motion-sick. One of those affected leaned out of the window and disgorged the contents of his stomach. Bull's eye! Loud cheers ensued. The hero smiled a sickly smile, the applause from his mates not fully compensating for the roiling discomfort in his belly.

'What on earth was that?'

The acolyte seated in front knew and had been hoping that he wouldn't be asked.

'Some bottles, followed by paan. That last bit looks like vomit, Poojya Guruji.'

'What the... What is going on? Who are all these people? Where are they going?'

'Poojya Guruji, it looks as though these buses all belong to the Sundarambal Transport Company.'

'Sundarambal? *That* Sundarambal?'

A moment's silence. 'I'm afraid so.'

'Are you telling me that...that...'

'I'm afraid so, yes. They are probably...most likely... headed for the function you are gracing. There are full-page adverts in all the local newspapers...'

'My name and photograph appear prominently, I assume?'

'Actually, Poojya Guruji...'

'I thought we had agreed that this would be a non-negotiable condition for my appearance.'

'We had. But these people...they can be so unreasonable...'

'Are all the people here like this?'

'Not all...'

'I just wish someone had told me all of this earlier. I'm disappointed with the advice I have been given. Very disappointed indeed. In any event, I suppose I can look forward to a quiet evening at the retreat once I'm done with all of this.'

The acolyte didn't reply.

There was relief as the AICTE visiting committee drove out to their final stop: the Sundarambal Institute of Management. Relief that they were almost done, that they were through with inspection visits for a while at least, that they could finally go back to their jobs, their comfortable niches, their familiar routines.

Lost as they were in their own thoughts, it took them a while to see that they were sharing the road with a large number of buses bearing the Sundarambal Transport Corporation name. A quick glance at their folders confirmed that they were on their way to the eponymous management institute. But where were all these buses going? Their occupants did not look like students. A large number sat on the roof passing around what looked like bottles of hooch. Along with their fellow passengers seated inside, they appeared to be in extreme good humour. Every now and then a stream of paan or vomit issued forth from either the roof or the windows. There was much backslapping and bonhomie and the extreme summer heat did nothing to curb the boisterous throng.

The members of the visiting committee wondered just what was going on. There appeared to be Sundarambal buses wherever they looked. Theirs seemed to be the only non-Sundarambal vehicle in sight.

Their driver, one eye on the barrelling buses, the other on the increasingly frequent splats of paan and vomit soiling his windshield, took a moment to answer their queries.

'Sir, big ceremony.'

'What ceremony?'

'Dr Rakshasan, big leader, he is having big ceremony. You see these buses? They are taking his followers to the ceremony.'

'These Sundarambal buses?'

'Yes, yes. Sundarambal Transport, Sundarambal University, Sundarambal TV, Sundarambal everything belongs to Dr Rakshasan. Sundarambal being his mother. Like a good son he has named everything after his mother. His mother cooked him excellent *kathirikai*, er...what you people are referring to as brinjal, and he is expressing his gratitude all his life. Very good son, he is, sir.'

Hota looked worried. 'Are you sure our visit to the Sundarambal Institute is today?'

'Yes, sir. It is on our schedule and they have been duly notified as per the guidelines.'

'Hopefully this big ceremony is in some other part of the university. This Sundarambal University, is it very big?'

'Yes, sir. Very big. Many thousands of students. They are coming from North India, Nepal, so many other places. All are coming here and creating troubles.'

'Troubles? What do you mean.'

'Sir, they are not understanding Tamil, they are not liking our food, they are liking our girls and they are creating problems. So much so that town people complained to Dr Rakshasan. He listened to all the problems and took action. These leaders, they are quick in taking action. But every action has a reaction. So now we have other problems.'

'What other problems?'

'First he created Sundarambal Security Services to control students from the north. They are given lathis, sickles and other weapons and soon students are under control. Going to class, eating idlis and not playing holi. But you see, sir, *our* youths are not wanting jobs in Sundarambal Security Services. They want BPO jobs, IT jobs, jobs in Chennai, politician jobs, film jobs and so on. So what does our Dr Rakshasan do? He gets security fellows from North India, Nepal and so on.' The driver lowered his voice and looked at them conspiratorially. 'In fact, some people are saying that these North Indian students who are finishing their studies here are getting job placements in Sundarambal Security Services. Under the Sundarambal job guarantee scheme. So now you have these security fellows who are not understanding Tamil, they are also not liking our food, they are liking our girls, they are playing holi, they are carrying lathis and sickles and they are creating problems. Big problems. Some people are now saying, this big ceremony is because Dr Rakshasan is afraid of losing elections because of all these problems. So he is having big ceremony. Plenty of beer, brandy, Pan Parag and biryani to make everyone happy. That is why all this vomit and spitting and nuisance. Big problems, sir, if you are asking me.'

Decision-making in a Chaotic World II

The director had been turfed out of his office: P.K. had set up his operations centre there and had commandeered Jagan's space as well. Jagan himself had been co-opted and was now scurrying around as one APA after another shouted out orders.

As the overseer, P.K. had concerns that were less earthbound. The unending line of buses snaking into the campus, the happy hordes emanating therein intent on exploring their surroundings and the displaced students scurrying around the vast campus meant billowing clouds of dust. Returning this unruly, amorphous and undisciplined cloud to earth was his primary preoccupation. Leader didn't like dirt. Nor did he like dust. He disliked anything that left any sort of mark on his starched white garb. Leader liked to be photographed gazing thoughtfully at distant horizons, aquiline nose preferably in profile. Anything that obscured those horizons disturbed his thoughts. Disturbances in the even tenor of Leader's thoughts had consequences. Bringing the dust down to earth would ensure that P.K. would not have to deal with those consequences.

The APAs had equally pressing concerns. Freed from the confines of their buses, masses of Leader's followers had converged on the imposing walls of the Dr Rakshasan Library to relieve themselves. Others found in the newly painted walls an ideal canvas for spray-painting psychedelic paan patterns. Leader liked starched white walls. He was unlikely to appreciate his followers' efforts at adding colour to their surroundings. Dissuading the followers was a delicate task. At this important moment, Leader needed them more than they needed him. In their current frame of mind, they asked not what they could do for their leader; they wanted to know what he could do for them. They were quick to grasp the ebb and flow of human fortunes and were determined to make the most of the moment.

There was another issue. In constructing his educational edifice, Dr Rakshasan's keen sense of the bottom line had led him to minimize the space devoted to bathrooms and toilets. Bathrooms and toilets cost money and did not bring in revenues. His efforts at securing the Deemed University status had been driven in part by a desire to arbitrage the regulatory demands of the UGC and the local parent university with respect to toilet space.

Adding 50,000 well-fed and well-watered supporters to a campus filled with students and barely adequate toilet facilities presented the harried APAs with a managerial challenge they were unable to cope with.

The supporters who had been persuaded away from the inviting walls of Dr Rakshasan Library found that the suggested alternatives offered limited scope for their activities. The distinctions between the pots, wash-basins and bathing areas were not evident to them, leading to rather predictable outcomes. The second-floor ladies' washroom at the Sundarambal Institute of Management, on which the director had lavished his attention, had more than its fair share of (exclusively male) visitors. The absence of the urinal which had offended AICTE did not bother them in the least. It just meant a larger space for target practice, a greater expanse in which to show off their individuality. This they did enthusiastically and noisily.

As Agarwal had demonstrated with his students, keeping the supporters fed and fuelled was a sure way of keeping them in good cheer. Leader liked happy followers and one group of APAs were tasked with ensuring that the caterer continued to churn out cauldrons of spicy biryani. All the canteens had been taken over and mounds of rice, spices, cut vegetables and dead chickens lay on the floor awaiting their turn in the cauldrons. Sundarambal Institute of Management's canteen had been commandeered as well. The caterers and the APA supervising matters there had no way of knowing that Rat Kill had been liberally applied around the floors.

Two of the Rat Kill victims had been interred in a cardboard box and now lay in a drawer in the director's desk, awaiting the AICTE team's scrutiny. The remaining evidence of the liberal application of Rat Kill – additional rats and other dead creatures occupying lesser positions in the hierarchy of living beings – had been cleared away.

Bereft of his office, the director was forced to stalk the corridors of his institute. Even without the milling crowds of supporters he was in unfamiliar territory. The quiet, air-conditioned confines of his office had been his home and refuge. Intrusions from a messy world could be contained and dealt with in those familiar surroundings. It gave him the space and time to regain that sense of calm equilibrium that was sine qua non of his existence.

Now, though, he was out in a noisy, uncertain world made worse by what was in store. He had to push through knots of rowdy, boisterous, crude fellows, intent on enjoying their day in the sun. A fastidious man who did not relish contact with the hoi polloi, he gingerly sidestepped the varied obstacles that marked the passage of Leader's followers. There was little point in remonstrating with them: they were unlikely to listen given the mood they were in and all he would get for his troubles was a headache.

He decided, instead, to keep his focus on the AICTE team visit.

First stop, the library. He had taken care of the lacunae, the paperwork and documentary evidence were ready and while he was borderline contemptuous about the AICTE reps, he wanted to make an impression on the accompanying IAS officers. IAS fellows were useful people to know: they were the gatekeepers for various government committees and commissions. The director felt he could usefully contribute to these and the perks that came with the committees were, well, not exactly irrelevant.

He paid little heed to the rising hubbub of voices as he rounded the corner next to the library – there was enough noise all around thanks to the barbarian hordes and he had his mind on what he needed to do next. The semi-reverie ended abruptly as he entered the library. A group of followers, relieved after their sojourn in the second-floor ladies' restroom, had discovered the library. In particular, they had discovered an advert in one of the magazines featuring a scantily clad lady. News of this discovery had been loudly and repeatedly announced and there was now a frenzied search for more of the same.

Mrs Gopalan was in hysterics as magazines and books were ripped apart and flung aside. Frustrated at their inability to find any more hidden gems, the mob was turning violent and overturning tables and chairs. Inspired by scenes from Lok Sabha TV, some were flinging chairs across the room while others tried to knock down magazine racks.

'Sir, look at these rowdies!' Mrs Gopalan screamed at the director.

The director was too busy gaping at the wreck of his beloved library to respond. He ducked as a book flew towards him and suddenly found his voice. 'Stop it, you bastards! Motherfucking louts! Get out! Get the hell out of here!' He flung the book back and caught a follower flush on the face.

There was a loud roar of anger as the follower yanked out a knife he had tucked away for contingencies like these. 'Which son of a dog dares to attack me?'

His mates, distracted from their fruitless search for scantily clad ladies by this call to arms, responded in kind. Knives were clearly the argument settling device of choice among them, but variety in the form of guns, sickles and even a sword quickly made itself evident. The relative merits of pens and swords might well have been debated in the rough neighbourhoods where the followers congregated, but the outcome was clear. The director, a Parker 61 tucked into his pocket, was outnumbered, out-knifed, out-sworded and outgunned. Mrs Gopalan's hysterics had abruptly collapsed into barely audible whimpers. The two shrank back, both eyeing the exit which now seemed a long way off.

The director attempted a discreet shuffle towards the exit. He was noticed.

'You! Did you throw the book? Where do you think you are going?'

'No. I only read books, I don't throw them. I need to go to the bathroom.'

'Me, too,' squeaked Mrs Gopalan, 'urgently.'

'Lady, you may leave,' barked the gent with the sword. 'You!' The weapon was now pointing accusingly at the director whose bladder was threatening a public embarrassment. 'Who are you?'

'I...I...I am the director of this institute. This is... was...my library.'

'We want pictures like this. This is your library, you can find the pictures. Now!' He brought his sword down on a table to reiterate his demand.

The director quickly went down on his knees to rummage through the torn magazines lying scattered about the floor. He was keenly aware of the tip of the sword tracing random arabesques a few inches away and his hand shook as he shuffled through the pages. He glanced at the door, his befuddled brain attempting to work out the respective odds against a quick dash or a slow crawl to freedom. Meanwhile, there was enough material strewn on the floor to keep his hands busy. His knees and back, unused to the stresses they were experiencing, added their protests to his bladder's.

His sluggish mind eventually registered some alien noises coming from the corridor outside. Running footsteps, raised voices and shouted orders came closer in a hurry and entered the library. It was Jagan at the head of a posse of uniformed security types. The director's dull eyes registered the Sundarambal logo on their uniforms.

'Sir, sir, what are you doing on the floor?'

'They asked me to search for...for...'

Jagan held up a large medallion with a stylized representation of Dr Rakshasan and waved it at the armed mob of followers. 'This man is our man,' he shouted. 'Why are you making him kneel? I shall inform Leader of this insubordination.'

Sword, sickles and knives shrank back as Jagan moved in.

'Can I...bathroom, please,' whimpered the director.

Jagan fished around in his pocket and pulled out another medallion. 'Keep this with you, sir. Hold it in front of you and you won't be troubled. I will see you outside.'

Clutching the medallion as a shield and hanging on to his crotch to avert a public humiliation, the director ran towards the nearest urinal.

Not too far away, the faculty was in conclave.

'Have you received an invitation for the function?'

'Invitation? Three times, maybe more, my scooter almost got hit by those buses. We are faculty of this institute. Forget invitations, even a little bit of respect they are not giving.'

'Yes, they should have supplied AC buses for the faculty.'

'If they are going to create such a disturbance, at least they could have given us leave. All my casual leave has been exhausted and I had to breathe all that smoke and dust.'

'As I said, AC buses for the faculty.'

'Even in our normal parking spaces, riff-raff are urinating and vomiting. Where are we supposed to park? There are buses everywhere and I had to go to that side, you know, near the Arts College, to park, and those Arts College students were sitting on the wall and spitting on me.'

'AC buses for the faculty would have solved the problem.'

'They are all rowdies, those Arts College fellows. I am ashamed to share the campus with them.'

'But many have joined our institute. Does that make us a rowdy institute as well?'

'So none of us has received an invitation for the function.'

'Thank God for small mercies. Imagine sitting with those rowdies. I'd rather wear a banian than sit with them.'

'That is not the point, madam. The point is that as respectable members of the institute, the same institute which is conferring a doctoral degree on the chancellor as per our original suggestion, let us not forget, courtesy demands that we at least get an invitation. Actually, given that the degree was our suggestion, we should have got VIP seats for the occasion.'

'And AC buses for transportation.'

'With VIP seats and AC buses, no need for Thilaka madam to wear banian either.'

'That was a sexist, derogatory remark and I demand that you withdraw it immediately.'

'Joke only, kindly excuse.'

'That was in very poor taste. How do you expect me to maintain faculty solidarity when I'm bombarded with base, insulting, humiliating pathetic apologies for jokes? Enough! I have better things to do than to waste my time listening to this drivel. All we do is talk. Does anyone care about what we say or what we think? Do you think any resolution we come up with is going to have the slightest impact on anyone? Enough! I'm going home.'

'If they had provided AC buses, so much more comfortable your trip home would have been.'

'But then with all of us present Professor Sambandham would not be able to get down at your stop.' The words had slipped out involuntarily and Nilakantan now shrank back, fearful of what was to come.

Thilaka had frozen upon hearing the words. She turned around slowly and very deliberately walked towards her cowering colleague.

'Stand up, you pusillanimous *paapaan*.'

Avoiding eye contact, Nilakantan pretended he hadn't heard. The slap, when it came, was unexpected and carried a sting.

'I said stand up, you cowardly, creepy piece of crap.'

Nilakantan stood up and was rewarded by two more slaps. Pent up rage overflowed the boundaries decreed by Thilaka's sex and social convention. With a yell of rage she began to pummel and scratch Nilakantan who quickly bent over into a protective, fetal crouch. Stunned for a moment, the rest of the faculty found their voices.

'Madam, please.'

'Gandhiji advocated non-violent resolution of disputes.'

'Gandhiji was never insulted by shitheads like him,' shouted Thilaka, punctuating her words with a series of well-delivered rights. 'If he had, he would have done this to that fool Jinnah.' She tried to bite Nilakantan and was foiled only by the shifting contours of Nilakantan's midriff. Undeterred by the shouts of protest from her faculty colleagues, she lunged forward once more, teeth bared and an angry growl emanating from depths where feral feelings seethed.

'Excuse me, but we were told that the faculty were meeting here.'

The IAS officers and the AICTE team had arrived.

Image Management I

Dr Rakshasan had arrived as well.

As a young man Dr Rakshasan had waited hours in blazing sunshine and pouring rain to pay his political dues. It was payback time now. He had, over many years, learned some home truths about politics, politicians and respect as he made his way through life. One in particular was that pain equals respect. Followers were expected to wait, and in turn, they respected leaders who made them wait. So 50,000 odd followers, assorted sidekicks, the joint chancellor, P.K., the director, Poojya Guruji and three wives – all of them waited for the Leader.

Secondly, followers respected ostentation. Dr Rakshasan had seriously considered an S-class Mercedes and a long wheelbase 7 series BMW as his preferred mode of surface transportation. Having seen a Maybach parked outside his favourite Amsterdam brothel, he decided that nothing less merited his consideration. He had substituted the hood ornament with an elaborate one made of Swarovski crystal; the door handles had been gold-plated; his smiling visage adorned the doors, bonnet and trunk lid, and a non-functioning radar array (gold-plated) rotated atop the roof.

Under normal circumstances, this should have been sufficient ostentation for his followers and the mere sight of the rotating radar enough to send them into frenzied raptures. But the biryani and booze and the hot winds had dulled their senses. One group, having inadvertently ingested Rat Kill along with their biryani, were in agony and their distress was making itself heard over the general commotion. Enthusiasm at the Leader's arrival had taken a backseat to more pressing concerns.

The group on stage were also experiencing discomfort. Portable air-conditioners had been put in place for the dignitaries. There was a problem, though. As Dr Rakshasan made his way through life, he had begun to understand that the more you had, the more you had to lose. Finding ways to get around this immutable law had become an obsession. His Vaastu consultant had informed him that east was a life-giving direction (the sun rose in the east and the rest followed as a natural corollary). Any stage he sat on therefore faced east. But May in Coimbatore meant hot winds blowing from the east. The air-conditioners, impressive tonnage notwithstanding, were inadequate in the face of nature's warm exhalations. Poojya Guruji and his three wives, wilting in the heat and sweating profusely, were no longer waiting eagerly for the big man's arrival.

The joint chancellor and P.K. perked up seeing the familiar outline of the rotating radar. It had been a long, hot, fraught morning. Things could, and did, go wrong, and P.K. had learned to plan for assorted contingencies. This event had had more than its fair share of stresses, not least having to transport and amuse 50,000 hooligans, but even that, at a stretch, could be seen as part of a day's work. He glanced back and glared at the director, in the dog house once P.K. had opened a drawer and seen two dead rats in their little coffin. The link to the writhing and shouting followers had been established soon thereafter. With idiots like this around, how on earth was he expected to ensure that the function went off without a major incident? The director, guessing the tenor of P.K.'s thoughts, kept a safe distance away and tried to ensure that he was not in P.K.'s direct line of sight.

The hot sun did little to improve P.K.'s state of mind. He wanted to wrap his fingers around the director's neck and squeeze the life out of him. The glint of the rotating radar meant relief of some sort. At least the main feature could get under way now.

Modern politicians had learnt a thing or two from their imperial predecessors. It was not enough to make a grand appearance. A grand build-up to the grand appearance was needed.

Well before the Leader was actually seen on stage, loud music meant to evoke the grandeur and pageantry of the Chola kings blasted out of the loudspeakers.

Canned shouts hailing the Leader and his achievements along with alliterative adjectives extolling his myriad virtues rent the air. Those not overcome with a surfeit of booze, biryani and Rat Kill responded with the appropriate answering calls. The voice of 50,000 followers in full-throated harmony was missing, though. Both volume and harmony failed to please the Leader's discerning ear.

'What is this, P.K.? My followers are not happy with my humble achievement?'

'They are extremely happy, Leader. The biryani and all are also much appreciated.'

'Then why are they not telling me how happy they are? Happy followers mean a happy leader. These unhappy followers are making me very unhappy.'

An unhappy Leader was the last thing P.K. wanted. Happiness and unhappiness were like rivers flowing down from the exalted summit occupied by him. As they made their way down, they spread and engulfed larger and larger numbers, leaving rewards or destruction in their wake. P.K. needed to halt and maybe even reverse this little stream of unhappiness before it became a raging torrent.

'Sir, I will take care of it. Your followers' happiness will light up this function shortly.'

'I want my wives to see my followers' happiness when I step on the stage.'

Dr Rakshasan did not look very happy as he set off on an inspection tour of the campus. A frown accompanied his stride and he looked unimpressed at the architectural excesses that marked the campus.

P.K. turned around and caught the director's eye. 'You, get all your students here immediately. Inform them that they must cheer Leader at the top of their voices.'

'These are management students and we try to inculcate independence of thought and action...'

'I am saying this once only. Inform them that if the cheering is not satisfactory they will fail their exams and be liable for summary rustication.'

Sent off on a wholly unwelcome mission by P.K., the director wondered how on earth he was going to persuade anyone to join the cheerleaders at the chancellor's coronation.

A coronation it was going to be, as a crown had been added to the sword and the mace. The general consensus had been that the followers were more likely to grasp the significance of the day's ceremony if it was capped off, so to speak, with a glittering crown.

But that was still some time away. Meanwhile, given recent developments, the faculty were unlikely to accede to P.K.'s wishes, while the students had been given the day off. Actually, any right-thinking person would have made themselves scarce from the campus. The director's thoughts juggled between finding a cheering squad and what would happen to him if he returned empty-handed. It was a morose and depressed director who slunk around what was left of his beloved institute.

Attracted by loud cheerful voices he made his way to the auditorium, recently re-upholstered and air-conditioned in response to an earlier AICTE demand. Pandemonium reigned there. Agarwal's newly acquired students, ensconced in cushioned, air-conditioned comfort pending the admission formalities, were in good spirits. Cases of beer and choice North Indian delicacies from Gupta's kitchen fuelled the good times.

'Who are you?' the director asked a group dancing near the entrance.

'Munnabhai MBA,' shouted one prospective manager, to much appreciative applause.

'MBA, MBA!' his friends joined in in a rhythmic cheer. This went on for a few minutes.

'Where did you come from?'

'Meerut, Saharanpur, Panipat, Bulandshahr, Ghaziabad... We want to do MBA!'

'MBA, MBA!'

'Did Professor Agarwal bring you all here?'

'MBA, MBA!'

'Do you want admission here?'

'MBA, MBA!'

The director remembered that there was a megaphone in the auditorium kept handy for occasions like these. It took him a few minutes to get it connected and working.

'*Do you want admission here?*' Designed to deal with noisy Indian crowds, the megaphone did its job. The chanting slowed, stopped for a moment. Then, uncertainly at first, gathering force as thoughts took hold:

'Yes! We want admission! We want MBA!'

'MBA, MBA!'

'Then you need to come with me and when I give the signal, you must shout this at the top of your voices: Dr Rakshasan, *vazhgai*, *vazhgai*.'

Dr Rakshasan rolled of their tongues easily enough, but the intricacies of the Tamil '*zh*' sound eluded them completely. There was puzzled confusion and nervous chatter.

'Not possible, sir.'

'Technical difficulties we are having.'

'What for we need to shout all this?'

The director cast about and hit on an alternative. 'Okay, try this instead: Dr Rakshasan, jai ho, jai ho!'

'But why you are asking to follow you and shout all this?'

'Do you want admission here?'

'Yes, sir!'

'Do you want an MBA?'

'Yes, sir!'

'Then follow me and, when I give the signal, shout: Dr Rakshasan, jai ho, jai ho!'

'Then you are giving admission?'

'Yes, but only if you shout loud enough. Let me see what you boys can do.'

The lusty cheers were a favourable portent, both for the director's career prospects and the students' MBA prospects.

The director had given his signal. Eager for an MBA admission, the flower of Haryana and western UP's youth bellowed forth their chant. The *Slumdog* chant caught the ear of the Leader's followers just as it had the Oscar voters and it was soon echoing throughout the pandal.

The Leader was sighted approaching the stage and the volumes surged in response. The frown gave way to a smile and by the time he was on stage the Leader was in good enough humour to greet his followers with a broad grin.

P.K. scurried around the stage making sure that all the actors knew their part in the choreographed pantomime to follow. This was as much political theatre as it was an ego boost to the Leader. It wasn't enough for it to be stage-managed without a hitch. The atmosphere had to be just so, as also the subtle details that would provide a certificate of authenticity to the followers. Against all expectations that idiot director had delivered – the rhythmic chant now threatened to bring down the pandals and exposing his dentistry to public scrutiny was something the Leader rarely did. Now, though, the onus was on him.

Having caught everyone's eye P.K. nodded at the Leader's young wife. As an added reminder, she was gently poked in her derriere with the sword. She flung herself with alacrity at the feet of junior wife, who blessed her with the air of a gracious goddess. The two of them together bent down before senior wife. Secure in her status as *primus inter pares*, with the added benefit of being the mother of Leader's eldest son, senior wife delivered her benediction with an air of condescension that befitted her status. Blessings she had in plenty and she could afford to be generous. The followers roared with approval at this display of family unity. The three ladies then moved towards the man of the moment.

To do so they had to get past Poojya Guruji, who rose as they approached, assuming that his blessings would be as sought after here in Coimbatore as they were in Delhi. P.K. frowned. This was not part of the programme. Worse, having the Leader's wives touch the feet of a Brahmin would have serious political ramifications. He glanced at the sword man. The tip of the sword burrowed hard into Poojya Guruji's shoulder, forcing him back into his seat. Guruji turned pale and tense with anger, but there was little he could do other than sit down and avoid P.K.'s angry glare.

The three wives, eyes downcast and looking as demure as middle age would allow them, bowed deeply, namasted and, in reverse chronological order, prostrated themselves before their master. It was a proud moment, a significant one for Dr Rakshasan and he milked it for all it was worth. He tried to imagine what a Chola king would have done in similar circumstances. His actual knowledge of the Cholas would not have stood up to scrutiny, but he had been an enthusiastic connoisseur of Tamil mythologicals in his youth and essayed an imitation of Sivaji Ganesan. He looked like a middle-aged turkey nodding its head. His followers, though, had watched the same movies as their leader and made the connection immediately. They went wild.

The slogan-shouting had flagged but now resumed with added vigour and enthusiasm. Agarwal's students were ensuring that there could be no reason to deny them their MBA seats. Besides, this was fun. Their coaching centres had briefed them on what to expect in their MBA interviews and group discussions. They had swotted up random facts and current managerial trends from their preparatory books. They knew all the CEOs of the Nifty 50. They knew about Al Gore and climate change. They knew the name of the speaker of the state assembly of Mizoram. They were familiar with arguments for and against multinationals. Now they knew that all of this had nothing to do with a managerial career. All they needed was lung power and that magic mantra: 'Dr Rakshasan, jai ho, jai ho!'

P.K. knew there could be too much of a good thing. He also knew that voices had their limits and that continued vocal backing would be needed as the ceremony proceeded. He nodded once more, this time catching Leader's eye. Dr Rakshasan bent low, patting his wives' heads in turn and bidding them to rise, but they knew the drill and kept their noses buried in the carpet until the tap of P.K.'s sandal told them otherwise.

Team Building

'So there are regular team-building exercises for the faculty?'

The completely unexpected entry of the AICTE team and the IAS officers had abruptly forced the faculty to turn their attention to the common enemy. There had been a moment or two when there had been shocked silence, when they were too stunned to react.

On its part the inspecting team had been lulled into expecting only the expected. Even their travails on the road to the campus and the long trudge across the campus to the institute hadn't primed them for anything other than the commonplace. The shock when they interrupted the faculty conclave was mutual.

'Is this the faculty room?' one of the IAS officers had asked hesitatingly.

Thilaka had been the first to recover. 'Yes, this is the faculty room. We are participating in a bonding exercise.'

'So...you are...this is...the faculty room?'

'Of course it is. I just told you so. Does it look like the library or canteen to you?'

'No, no. It is just that when we came in it looked as though you were about to...'

'As I said, this was a bonding exercise.'

'Oh. Ah. A bonding exercise.'

'A team-building exercise, in other words.'

'So there are regular team-building exercises for the faculty?'

'Haven't you heard of outward-bound programmes where corporate executives participate in team-building exercises?'

'Well, yes, but it looked as though you were about to...'

'You thought I was going to bite him?'

'Well, it certainly looked as though...'

'What do you take me for, a dog?'

'No, no...'

'A bull dog? A Rottweiler? A Rajapalayam?'

'What was that again?'

'Rajapalayam. You have never heard of Rajapalayams?'

'No...but...'

'And you fancy yourself a dog lover?'

'As a matter of fact, I do like dogs, but what has that...'

'Lhasa Apsos, Chihuahuas, Dalmations, Alsatians, any of them ring a bell?'

'Of course. What do you take me for?'

'I'm just getting to that. Where are Chihuahuas from? Alsatians? Lhasa Apsos?'

'Chihuahua, Alsace, Lhasa, of course. I was on the Stephen's quiz team. But I suppose all of you here would know nothing about Stephen's.'

'Listen, Mr Stephens. Whether or not my colleagues and I have heard about Stephen's is completely besides the point. You don't know what a Rajapalayam is. I suppose you are not even aware that there is a town here in Tamil Nadu called Rajapalayam. And I know for certain that you haven't a clue that there is a breed of dog originating in that town bearing that name. You asked me what I take you for. I'll tell you. You are a bloody idiot. Not just that. You are an arrogant, opinionated, snobbish North Indian who thinks nothing of substance exists south of the Vindhyas and that all people here do is bite other people. Any more of this and I'll turn you over to that mob outside, letting them know that you referred to Tamilians as dogs.'

'I did no such thing! This is a misunderstanding...'

'Who are you anyway and what do you and your buddies want?'

'I am Santosh Hota, an IAS officer from the HRD ministry. This is my colleague Akshay Sinha. These gentlemen are from AICTE. We are here to inspect your institute.'

'ID?'

The AICTE representatives looked at each other and their IAS cohorts. It hadn't occurred to them that their bona fides would be questioned, least of all by someone from an institute they were inspecting. Deference and servility were expected, yes, but not in-your-face aggression.

'We are the inspectors. Our visit has been duly communicated to the authorities...'

'How do we know that you are not municipal dog catchers?'

'Or rat catchers?'

'Look, here is a copy of our communication of the fifth instance, and here are the files pertaining to the aforementioned inspection...'

'Let me see that.' Anbuchezian snatched the file away.

'Wait, wait. Those files contain confidential information and disclosure of the same without prior permission is prohibited via Section 26 of the Act.'

'Look,' said Anbuchezian ignoring the implications of ignoring the provisions of the Act, 'rats. On top itself. These bloody fellows are interested only in the rats.'

'What rats?' Hota wanted to know.

'Did you mug up rat categories for your quizzing career?'

'I beg your pardon! What on earth are you talking about?'

'You wanted to know what rats. Does it make any difference what rat it is?'

Bewildered, Hota shook his head. 'What on earth is going on? What is all this about rats?'

'In our previous inspection, it was observed that two numbers of rats were present in the canteen. A recommendation was made to the institute to correct said lacunae prior to the subsequent inspection which is now currently underway.' As always, the AICTE representatives had the facts on their fingertips.

'I thought we were here to evaluate educational standards.'

'Under the provisions of the Act, any uncorrected lacuna renders the subject institution liable for de-recognition after due notice.'

'So what are we supposed to do about…about this lacuna as you call it?'

'It is incumbent on the said institution…'

'Rats are the director's responsibility.'

'What?'

'The director has taken responsibility for the rats.'

'Excuse me, but are you telling me that the *director*, the head of this institute, is responsible for *rats*?'

Agarwal was quick to spot the reasons for the Sinha's confusion. 'Flat organization structure here. No hierarchy. Shared responsibility. Practice what we preach. Hence rats are director's responsibility. Teaching is faculty's responsibility. Learning is student's responsibility. Shared responsibility as per flat organization structure.'

Sinha gaped. 'You mean you actually put these ideas, these concepts, into practice?'

'Mintzberg is always talking about effective management.' As ever, Sambandham had bided his time and intervened when he felt the moment was right. This time, even Thilaka was left slack-jawed at Sambandham's evocation of Mintzberg.

Things had not been the same for Sambandham ever since Dakshayini had left her proposal for the conference with him. Her face, her smile, the way she said 'Sir', that self-conscious walk as she entered his room: all had roused in him emotions that Thilaka's more forward approach had failed to excite. She appeared in his dreams at night, she was a major distraction during the day. Each day he waited for her to come and fine-tune the conference agenda, disappointment weighing him down as the hours tolled without her sweet smile gracing his office and rejuvenating his life. One day he decided that her words would suffice even if her presence was not forthcoming. He read her proposal, slowly and without comprehension at first, more quickly but still without comprehension later. Repeated exposure to the words burnt them into his memory. They were a balm to his troubled feelings. The knowledge that he could now exchange thoughts with her when she did show up gave the words added significance. By the time the AICTE team arrived, he had memorized the entire proposal and could regurgitate paragraphs, phrases and acronyms with ease.

'Mintzberg has critiqued traditional management education,' he went on, 'for not paying attention to the human aspects of decision-making and management. Management is not just about models. Human interactions are key to successful management and organizational structures are key to successful human interactions.'

'Mintzberg? Did I hear you say Mintzberg?'

Sambandham was on a roll and was not to be denied by a mere IAS officer. 'Human interactions are key when considering the relationships companies have with the societies they operate in. Traditional management education with its reliance on models and statistics ignores these aspects according to Mintzberg.'

'Truer words have never been spoken,' chimed in Thilaka, a light of realization shining in her eyes. 'We at the Sundarambal Institute of Management believe that creating effective managers is a calling above all others. We need to set an example that our students can emulate. This bonding exercise that we are undertaking ensures that the Sundarambal faculty see themselves as a team, not as random individuals being pulled hither and thither by random centrifugal forces. We impart education as a team. We are not dogs.'

'Of course you are not dogs. That was just a misunderstanding as I've already said and my apologies for that. More importantly, though, I take it that Henry Mintzberg's ideas find due expression in your courses.'

'Of course,' said Thilaka who in reality had no idea who this Mintzberg fellow was.

'Also ideas of Thiruvalluvar,' added Nilakantan.

'And Periyar,' piped in Anbuchezian.

'Our students are exposed to a variety of concepts and ideas.'

'But as per inspection guidelines correction of lacunae is the primary responsibility of institutions undergoing inspection vide…'

'Let's go see the director about that. This has been a most fascinating discussion, and I'd like to continue it once we are done with the director. Perhaps we can ask him to join us. Team-building activities for faculty. I have to tell you, professors, that no one on our current round of inspections has suggested anything remotely as interesting. Fascinating, indeed. And please accept my personal apologies. I have to say that I never expected this level of involvement with modern management ideas in this corner of the country.'

'I can also talk about the role of the board of directors in formulating corporate social responsibility guidelines in the oil and gas industries.' Sambandham was annoyed at Thilaka for interrupting just when he was getting into his stride and wanted to ensure he had the last word.

'Of course, of course. My colleagues have their checklist to deal with, so, if we can finish with the director and the rats, we can continue.'

They trooped down to the director's office.

P.K. and his team had left the director's office to take their places at the Leader's convocation. The dead rats had been left on the table.

'There. Two dead rats. Satisfied?'

Hota looked the other way while Sinha wondered what sequence of events had brought him face to face with two dead rats in a distant suburb of Coimbatore. The AICTE officer peered at the rats, then picked up a pencil and nudged them. No reaction.

'Two numbers rats, dead,' he said to himself as he made a note in his file.

His colleague flipped through his papers. 'Our communication clearly indicated that the rats, two numbers as already indicated, had to be killed in a humane manner using an AICTE-approved killer. Kindly provide confirmation.'

Feet were shuffled, throats cleared, the sounds of people waiting for someone else to break the silence filled the room.

Agarwal finally spoke. 'The only ones to know if humane methods were used are the rats themselves. And since the rats are dead we shall never know.'

Dead silence. This logical dog had swallowed its tail and successfully stumped the fine minds of the IAS, AICTE and the rest of the Sundarambal faculty.

'One minute, please. In addition to the two numbers of rats, now deceased as per our inspection, the person or persons concerned jointly or severally responsible for the demise of the said rats will be able to clarify the manner and humaneness of said demise.' Mere logical conundrums were not about to stop the AICTE inspectors on their appointed rounds.

'Director is responsible for the rats. He has even provided a nice box for the dead rats indicating his humane approach and love for dead animals.'

'Mintzberg has stressed the humane approach in the formation of corporate teams and the importance of teamwork in the pursuit of corporate goals.'

'Do you think the rats and the director formed a team to implement their humane demise?'

'What on earth is going on? What do teams and Mintzberg have to do with these rats? Why is AICTE obsessed with rats?'

'As per…'

'Hold on. Wait a minute. Where is the director? Let's just ask him and move on to more relevant matters.'

'Director is at the function. Chancellor function.'

'I've had enough of these rats. Let's go and find the director.'

Image Management II

The director was nowhere to be seen as the inspection team entered the sprawling area covered by the shamianas. Voices – massing in unison at times and breaking into a babble of individual arguments at others – rose and fell in gigantic waves. Martial music could be dimly heard through the general din. A vast, smelly sea of humanity – squatting, standing, spitting, vomiting, shouting, writhing, groaning, attending to itching crotches and armpits, dancing, drunkenly lurching – stretched as far as the eye could see. There was a stage in the distance.

'Look! Do you see what I see?'

They followed his arm to the stage. Three ladies, who looked extremely bored, were fanning away the heat as best as they could, along with an expressionless, bearded man clad in saffron. Security guards looked nervously at the rabble below them. Factotums tried to keep the ladies and gent in good humour.

'Is that really our old friend, Poojya Guruji?'

'What on earth is he doing here?'

'Shit! I thought we came here to get away from him!'

'And that fellow behind him...what the hell is he carrying?'

'A sword and... good lord, I haven't seen that sort of thing since the *Mahabharata* TV show...a mace?'

'Poojya Guruji doesn't look too happy.'

'I'm glad he's the one getting some grief. Makes for a nice change.'

'Who are these people anyway? Faculty team-building, then Mintzberg, and now they have Poojya Guruji at the wrong end of a sword. I've heard even the PM doesn't take liberties with him, and look what these jokers are doing to him.'

'There is something distinctly odd about this whole setup. This lot on the one hand and that Mintzberg-spouting chappie on the other. There is some disconnect somewhere.'

These ruminations were interrupted by noisy shouts from a fresh lot of supporters. They looked different: jeans, stylishly unkempt hair, affected swaggers, a non-South Indian look and feel. When intelligible, they sounded distinctly non-Tamilian. They followed the direction of the chants. Their gaze finally rested on a portly man clad in white, who looked extremely pleased.

'Is his hair real?'

'What about that moustache? How does he eat?'

'Forget eating. Do you think he has ever kissed any of those ladies?'

'Who are those ladies?'

'Do you think they enjoy kissing him?'

'There could be many a hair between lip and lip.'

'I can't figure out where Poojya Guruji fits into all this.'

Poojya Guruji's mind was occupied by similar thoughts. Yes, he knew what he had been told to do, he knew he didn't like any of it one bit, his acquaintance with the business end of the sword meant that there was no alternative to going through with the whole business. But why did they need him? Based on everything he'd seen so far there were two points to this whole show: an ego boost to the mustachioed thug and entertainment for the assembled masses. They were a disgusting lot. Along with all the noises and shouting, assorted smells – none whatsoever pleasant – wafted over the stage. What they needed were dancing girls in short skirts shaking their bottoms to locally popular film songs. The cruder the better. Why did they need him, with his refined sensibilities, his otherworldly concerns and his sophisticated circle of friends and disciples? This was terrible. Once back in Delhi, he would have a word with the PM. These two-bit politicians needed reminding from time to time of their place in the world. Nothing like some prime ministerial muscle to put them back where they belonged. Lost in his thoughts, Poojya Guruji missed his cue.

P.K. had nodded. When that didn't work, he gestured at Dr Rakshasan's feet, which were tapping impatiently, unnoticed by Poojya Guruji. Accustomed to making others wait while he thought his thoughts, he had allowed his mind to wander. Finally the sword interrupted the flow of his thoughts and reminded him where he was and what he was expected to do. Reluctantly, he got up.

Dr Rakshasan was a short man. This was not evident in the many posters and plywood cutouts bearing his countenance that graced all the towns and villages where his writ ran. These portrayed him in superhuman terms, towering over trees and lesser mortals and mere inches away from where assorted heavenly deities (political and religious) competed with each other to shower their blessings on him. His wives and the sidekicks who surrounded him in his staged appearances were all shorter than him, allowing him to sustain the illusion. P.K. had just noticed that Poojya Guruji was a tall man.

The sword dug into his shoulder as he straightened, forcing him into a stoop as he approached Dr Rakshasan. Bent over almost double, seething at the repeated insults, Guruji made his way to the appointed spot where a further nudge of the sword reminded him to prostrate himself before the Leader. There, with the sword pointedly reminding him of the realities of his situation, he was able to examine Dr Rakshasan's dirty, uncut toenails, his cracked heels, his swollen ankles and the gold-embroidered border of his *veshti* at leisure, as also the well-worn and never-cleaned carpet.

And the rat hiding under the lectern.

Poojya Guruji was musophobic. In other words, he hated rats. He tried to get up. The sword made its point. He subsided. The rat scurried over to make his acquaintance. He struggled against the sword. A Hawaii-chappalled foot added its weight to that of the sword. He subsided once more.

Poojya Guruji was dimly aware of loud cheering from the audience but the rat had him in thrall. The rat and Poojya Guruji eyeballed each other for a few minutes before it came over slowly for a closer look. Its whiskers twitched a few times before it rolled over and died.

Mere feet away, the entrepreneur behind Rat Kill allowed the warm waves of adulation to wash over him. What he knew, and what Poojya Guruji – unversed in the subtle symbolism of Tamil politics – didn't know, was that few Tamil politicians had been able to get a bona fide Brahmin to touch their feet. Add to that the fact that *this* Brahmin was a Hindi-speaking North Indian wrapped in saffron and a beard. The cheers from the mob and the grin on Dr Rakshasan's face were ample evidence that they recognized the moment's political significance. The moment was one to savour, its essence to be taken in with delicate sniffs and its flavours to be sampled nibble by nibble. The loud cheers were mere confirmation that the smells and taste had met with the followers' approval.

P.K. had planned on a minute or two for all of this. Popular demand stretched this closer to ten. P.K., in all likelihood, hadn't read Shakespeare but he knew a thing or two about dramatic tension. He let it build. He let the crowd and his boss indulge themselves. He let the drama reach its tipping point. Judging the moment to perfection, his sandals beat out a tattoo on the carpet.

Transfixed by the dead rat, Poojya Guruji saw neither this nor felt the absence of pressure from the sword and the Hawaii chappal. In happier times, watching life leave the rat might have prompted thoughts on the evanescence of life. In these unhappy moments, his thoughts centred on the lights wielded by the TV crews and the knowledge that his humiliation would soon be very public.

'Eleven minutes and...oh...roughly thirty seconds.'

'Did you get any shots? The boss is going to like this.'

'You know these mobiles...good for close-ups. But at this distance...'

'You can make out it is him, right?'

'Yes...But we should find out who those TV chappies are. They seem to have all the angles covered. Those press photographers as well. Nice, juicy close-ups.'

'I'd dearly love to see the expression on his face.'

'The next time Poojya Guruji convenes that committee of his, I think we should circulate this along with the minutes. This is most educative. I'm sure the McKinsey lot will want to get back on the committee once they see this.'

'I'm sure the boss will also change his mind about attending once he gets to hear about this.'

'And don't forget, this is a business school function. We now have new insights into management education and how management schools function.'

An irritated P.K. finally kicked Poojya Guruji in the ribcage and motioned to him to rise. Thoughts interrupted once more, Poojya Guruji rose slowly, victimhood weighing down his movements.

P.K. had given this segment of the ceremony much thought. He knew that the dazzle and glitter would leave a lasting impression on the followers. So, too, the public humiliation of the North Indian Brahmin. But would these drunken, semi-literate clods really understand the significance of what they were witnessing? They needed to understand that this was not just another political function, that this could not be put out of mind once the day was done like some flavour-of-the-week Kollywood blockbuster. This had the potential to spin the Leader's career into a more rarefied orbit and he needed to convey that clearly to the noisy mob that, aside from the Rat Kill group, was bubbling and frothing with a variety of happy emotions.

He had eventually decided that the direct, literal approach was best.

As Poojya Guruji rose, the royal Chola processional music stopped and the loudspeakers crackled and squealed in anticipation of an announcement. Agarwal's bunch, exhausted with their chanting and feeling that they had done enough to merit their MBA admissions, quietened down. Barring the Rat Kill group which was in a deep and noisy well of agony, the crowd of followers responded to the loudspeakers' promptings and eagerly awaited the next act of what was proving to be a most satisfactory outing.

'Today is a very special day. The day has dawned with the most auspicious of portents. The sun and the moon, Jupiter and Saturn, the stars adorning the heavens, the very universe, all are holding their breath. For today our dear Leader, our most respected and beloved Leader, our father and mother combined, the one who most graciously and generously shelters us under his wings, who looks after all our needs, who feeds and clothes even the most undeserving of his followers, this very leader is being accorded a very special honour.

'You will all have heard of Dr Newton, Dr Einstein, Dr MGR, Dr Karunanidhi and, of course, our very own leader, our dear leader, our most respected and beloved leader, Dr Rakshasan. He is one among many distinguished doctors. But today our Dr Rakshasan, our modest and accomplished Dr Rakshasan, our Dr Rakshasan with his three beautiful and obedient wives, our Dr Rakshasan who has created this university, the one and only Sundarambal University, named after his beloved mother, the mother goddess Sundarambal who has showered her munificence on this world by sharing with us humble followers her genius son Dr Rakshasan who, today, will attain something rare, something which even astronomers have not seen in their studies of the universe.

'Today, after deep deliberation and study, the Sundarambal Institute of Management has found an appropriate acknowledgment for the accomplishments of our Leader. Today, in just a few minutes, our Leader, Dr Rakshasan, will be accorded a signal honour.

Even Julius Caesar, Veerapandian Kattabhoman, Mahatma Gandhi and the Queen of England have not been accorded a similar honour. In just a few minutes, when the golden mace touches his immortal and knowledgeable shoulders, for the first time in the history of the universe, our Dr Rakshasan will become Dr Dr Rakshasan. Your very own leader, your protector and provider of tasty biryani will not be just Dr Rakshasan but Dr Dr Rakshasan!'

The voice, that of an oratorically gifted Kollywood actor, had risen to a crescendo. Fireworks, thoughtfully supplied by the Sundarambal Cracker Factory in Sivakasi, came in on cue, bursting in a cascade of deafening explosions.

The crowd, rising as one to the bait, erupted in cheers.

Managing the Regulator

The director had been walking around, making sure his flock stayed together and made the right noises. He was keen to catch P.K.'s eye but in the general noise and chaos he hoped that he had been able to catch P.K.'s ear at least. This was demeaning and well beneath his dignity but in these brash and materialistic times, he had to accept the compromises needed to keep his job. He moved with distaste along the fringes of the lumpen mob, an eye on the stage where the goings-on looked like some bizarre parody, meant for retards with mental age in the low single digits. He had signed the diploma under duress ('It is your institute which suggested this,' he had been told); he knew that the impressive looking parchment featuring his signature would soon be on display on all Sundarambal TV channels; he knew that some acquaintances from his better days would be calling to inquire about this particular turn in his fortunes.

He noticed an odd bunch on the periphery of the pandal. They kept a keen eye on the proceedings but clearly did not belong in this gathering. He stared at them for a few minutes before curiosity got the better of him.

'Excuse me, but you are not part of Dr Rakshasan's group, are you?'

Sinha and Hota looked at him with interest. 'And you are...?'

'I am the director of the Sundarambal Institute of Management and...'

'Oh, you are the rat person, then. Just the man we want to see.'

'I'm sorry, I didn't get your meaning. What is all this about a rat person? And who are you?'

'Well, we found these two dead rats in your office and these gentlemen here needed you to clarify certain aspects of their demise.'

'They are dead, AICTE wanted them dead, am I now supposed to compose a requiem for a dead rat, sorry, two dead rats, united in death as they no doubt were in life? Or am I permitted to outsource the composition of the said requiem to Ilayaraja or Rahman or some other musically talented animal lover to satisfy AICTE's boundless curiosity about their fate? I take it you are part of the inspection team?'

The AICTE rep had shuffled his papers and files and found the relevant provisions hereto. He cut in before the IAS gentlemen could respond.

'As per our communication, the said rats were to be killed by an AICTE-certified rat killer using humane means. Kindly provide documentary evidence of the same.'

'Does Mukesh Ambani kill rats using humane means by employing AICTE-certified rat killers?'

'As per the report of the AICTE-constituted inspection team as referred to herewith...'

'Did Dhirubhai Ambani kill rats using humane means by employing AICTE-certified rat killers?'

'As per the Act, we are not required to answer irrelevant questions posed in response to our queries...'

'Was Dhirubhai Ambani a successful businessman because of his rat-killing techniques? Do you even know whether Dhirubhai Ambani or Mukesh Ambani ever killed a rat? Do you even know if there are rats in the Reliance offices? What does any of this have to do with management? What does any of this have to do with education?'

'The Act states that...'

'Fuck your Act. I'm sick of your fucking Act. You can take your fucking Act and shove it up your fucking arse. Use your AICTE-certified act shover while you are at it. You know how much time I wasted looking for an AICTE-certified rat killer? I'm supposed to be running a bloody management institute for God's sake and here I was calling one bloody AICTE-certified rat killer after another and you know what? Your fucking list is fucking outdated!'

'Director, please calm down.'

'Why should I calm down? Does your bloody Act also specify that directors should calm down? Bloody easy for you to tell me to calm down. I have to deal with you and your bloody humane rat-killing questions.' He pointed at the stage. 'I have to deal with those bloody clowns and their bloody ceremony.' He nodded at the audience. 'I have to deal with these low-lives destroying the bathroom I had renovated on your orders. And you tell me to calm down?'

'Director…'

'Okay, I'll calm down as per your communication. Provided I get your permission in triplicate, I'll even compose that requiem myself. I'll even grant AICTE all rights to use that requiem to further the cause of management education in India. Generations of students will benefit. An army of Ambanis will march forth, clutching AICTE-recognized diplomas, taking India with them into the managerial future, singing my requiem as they march. Provided he gets AICTE permission, Mani Ratnam can film the whole bloody procession. Calmly, of course. As per the Act.'

The golden mace looked and felt cheap. Made of papier-mâché, crudely finished with gold paint and held together by sellotape, the mace was best appreciated at a distance.

A sullen Poojya Guruji hefted the mace and pondered the coming together of constellations that had led him to this pass. He thought for a moment of smashing it on the grinning bastard's head. After all, he had little left to lose now. On second thoughts, though, maybe not. This rabid mob would not take kindly to their leader's hairdo being disturbed by a fake mace. And the leader himself might not take kindly to the public revelation that the mace was a fake. Gritting his teeth, he went through the motions.

The left shoulder first, then the right, as he had been instructed. Gently, as the instructions had emphasized. It wasn't easy doing all this while on his knees, but he had, after all, suffered greater inconveniences as an itinerant sadhu in the Himalayas.

Then came the sword. Not the one that had dug into his back, but a cardboard cousin of the mace, wrapped in silver foil and made up to suggest a Chola provenance. The bastards were clearly taking no chances and didn't care that he was aware of the trust deficit. Left shoulder first, then the right. He wondered if it was all part of some pagan superstition, this business of leading with the left, or whether there was some political symbolism that he was missing. Just one more act, and his knees could relax a bit, a few more minutes, long minutes perhaps but minutes rather than hours, and he could be away from this and back in a world where he was master and had some control over his life.

He was handed a large platter with a scroll on it. A bright red ribbon held the scroll together. He noticed in a distracted fashion that the platter was silver and that he needed to get off his knees if he was to club the thug over the head with it. Instead, he bowed his head as he had been told to do and offered the scroll as if to a deity. The thug accepted the scroll with a look that combined indifference and condescension, undid the ribbon and displayed it to the crowd.

On cue, the loudspeakers burst into life: 'On this glorious day, in this fifty-fifth year of his glorious life, the humble management, director, faculty, employees and students of the glorious Sundarambal Institute of Management beg Dr Rakshasan, the glorious chairman, to accept this humble token of their esteem in honour of his glorious achievements in the field of management, this degree and title of Doctor of Management.'

A crown, gold-covered papier-mâché like the mace and studded with fake jewels like the sword, was placed on the platter.

Dr Dr Rakshasan's many followers cheered lustily as Chola ceremonial music blared forth once more. Dr Dr Rakshasan smiled modestly. Unlike Julius Caesar, he did not need further persuasion. He crowned himself and spoke into the mike. 'Now, I am Dr Dr Rakshasan.'

'The impugned degree is in violation of numerous sections of the Act. Under the provisions of the Act, a show cause notice is liable to be issued seeking explanations for each violation and outlining the penalties thereto should the said explanations not satisfactorily answer the questions referred to earlier.' The AICTE man had the prim look of a bureaucrat who had uncovered numerous violations of the Act.

'Fuck the Act.' The Director was not done with his commentary on the Act.

'What on earth are you talking about?' Violations of the Act were the provenance of junior bureaucrats and IAS officers' concerns rarely descended to these mundane details. Hota thought of himself as a big-picture person, impressed despite himself at what he had seen and heard at the Sundarambal Institute of

Management. The sight of Poojya Guruji's nose buried in the carpet for eleven minutes and thirty seconds had been a powerful one. It had the potential to change the face of management education in India. The path of progress was not to be derailed by some two-bit violation of the Act.

'Only an institution approved under Section 3 of the Act as a Deemed to be University is permitted to offer the doctoral degree. As per our records the Sundarambal Institute of Management has not been accorded recognition as a Deemed to be University. Furthermore, it might be noted that doctoral degrees are classified as either Doctor of Philosophy or Doctor of Science. There is no provision under the Act for the degree of Doctor of Management. The director of the institute, as the recognized signatory authority, shall be held liable under the provisions thereof.'

'I can be held liable if and only if a violation of the Act has been clearly established. Your statement that I *shall* be held liable indicates mala fides, *a priori* determination of outcomes, pre-judgement of the facts and a wilful disregard of due process. I have here a distinguished representative from the HRD ministry as a witness to these gross violations of departmental norms. Notwithstanding my earlier comments on the Act which were covered under the constitutional guarantees to free speech, I hereby claim protection on the grounds that the procedures laid out in the Act were violated by your statement. So what are you going to do now?'

Event Management

Dr Dr Rakshasan cleared his throat.

'Since I am now Dr Dr Rakshasan, my followers, my students, my teachers and many eminent people around the world have asked me to share my expertise in the field of management. I, of course, do not like to talk about myself, but when so many people are asking, what am I to do? Even my wives are asking, why don't you share this expertise you are having? We are hungry for your knowledge just like you are hungry for our cooking. What can I say, I am always hungry for my wives' cooking. Three wives I have, all are first-class cooks. Whenever I was looking for a new wife, first thing I was checking is how her cooking is. So my first wife, she makes excellent *vatha kuzhambu*, my second wife makes excellent *keerai koothu*, and my third wife makes excellent cauliflower manchurian.'

The wives looked pleased at being singled out for praise, while much of the gathered multitude responded cheerily at this display of marital harmony. Only a few dissenting voices from the Rat Kill section marred the discussion of the roles of domestic bliss and satisfied stomachs in ensuring managerial effectiveness.

'This biryani, it is killing me!' shouted an anguished voice.

'You are eating manchurian, why did we get this biryani?'

'I am going to die! You are giving us lectures, but we are all going to die! Leader, save us! Even God is not listening!'

'Are you going to take a fourth wife who can make proper biryani?'

Public happiness does not allow for dissent. Caught off guard just as he was getting into his stride, Dr Dr Rakshasan glared at P.K. It might have been a mere grain of sand in a sea of rice, but grains of sand had no place in Dr Dr Rakshasan's happy universe, and it was P.K.'s job to ensure that any errant grains of sand were blown away before they made their presence evident. He marched off, a monsoon's worth of wrath raging within, to deal with the Rat Kill troublemakers. He had fed them well, let them intoxicate themselves to their hearts' content, and been rewarded by wisecracks and enough grains of sand to make a bullock cart seize up: A few titters to begin with, some half-nervous laughter at the manchurian jibe, then genuine amusement – a ripple of laughter that flowed over the large crowd – when the fourth wife was mentioned.

P.K. was not amused. The Leader collected wives, P.K. dealt with their complaints. Having three wives was like having three children in one respect: the one in the middle could be safely ignored. A fourth wife meant intrigues. Intrigues spelt trouble. This needed to be nipped in the bud.

Thrown off stride, Dr Dr Rakshasan tried to regain the thread of his thoughts. 'As I was saying, chicken manchurian...'

'Cauliflower manchurian,' a loud voice in the audience issued a peremptory correction, to appreciative applause.

'Now look here, you have requested me to talk, so shut up and listen to what I am saying.'

'I have not asked you to talk so you should listen to what we are saying.' Thereby establishing a connection between alcohol, loose tongues and laughter.

'Mind it! I have given you food and all, now you have to listen to me. After all, I became Dr Dr Rakshasan because I listened to my leaders when I was like you. If you don't listen to me, you will all remain as you and only I will be me. And then, even ten years from now, you will be sitting there and having to listen to me.'

That got their attention. Career advice from politicians was rarely forthcoming. And when that advice outlined the alternatives in such stark terms, it needed to be taken seriously. The rumble of conversation died down.

'Do you know why I have become like this? Of course you don't. Because, if you did, you would have become like me and then I wouldn't have to tell you this. The secret is this. Look at this person here.' He pointed at the joint chancellor. Unnerved at being singled out, he made a beeline for the Leader's feet and flattened himself on the carpet. The dead rat was still there but he was too busy staring at his Leader's toenails to notice.

'This is the secret. Can any of you do this? This is leadership. This is management. Look at this.'

He raised his leg and wiggled his toes. The joint chancellor's forehead touched the toes several times. Without taking his eyes off the carpet he hauled himself up into a stoop and slowly backed off to his chair. Another toe wiggle and he sat down.

'See, this Chinese fellow Mao is saying that power comes from the barrel of a gun. He is wrong. Power actually comes from this.' He hiked up his *veshti* and wiggled his toe for the benefit of the audience. 'Real power comes from the toe of a leader. Now, all of you, shake your toe.'

Fifty thousand toes were shaken.

'Did anything happen?'

Puzzlement all around. It wasn't clear to anyone whether anything was supposed to happen. A low buzz of confused comment floated around.

'See? You are not leaders, so nothing happened. Now you come here.' He looked at Poojya Guruji whose knowledge of Tamil was non-existent and who was wondering just what these strange Madrasis were up to. The tip of the sword did the translation. The blade of the sword made sure he didn't rise above a stoop. 'Shake your toe,' commanded Dr Dr Rakshasan.

It took a few moments to clarify things and to get Poojya Guruji, still stooped, to raise a leg and wiggle a toe. The audience held their breaths and waited. Unmindful, the universe carried on with its business.

'See, he is wearing long hair, beard, all these saffron clothes but nothing happened. *He* is not a leader. *He* cannot teach you anything about management. That only *I* can. But if he has a proper haircut like me, and shaves properly like me, and eats *keerai koothu* like me, he can also slowly learn to become a leader. Like me. You see, these North Indians don't eat proper food. Some of them don't even shave. Like this fellow here. And they think they can become leaders just like that. In fact, I'll tell you why I asked this fellow to come here. I wanted to show you all that you can't become a leader just like that. There are plenty of these fellows running around, talking about leadership and management and so on. Don't listen to them. See this?'

He wiggled his toe once more and the joint chancellor sprang forward to pay obeisance once again. In his eagerness to get close to the fount of the Leader's power, he nudged Poojya Guruji. A football referee might have even dismissed it as incidental contact in the run of play. Poojya Guruji, stooped, balanced on one leg, his other leg extended at an angle in order to afford the audience an unobstructed view of his powerless toe, lost his balance and toppled over.

The audience cheered and rose as one in spontaneous applause at this successful demonstration of the Leader's leadership prowess.

P.K. knew that he couldn't control the Rat Kill dissenters by himself. He got a bunch of Sundarambal Security Services sorts to accompany him. They knew the drill:

browbeating uncooperative crowds, displaying muscle and protecting the Leader's interests were all part of a day's work. Restraint wasn't something they were familiar with. Gentle persuasion was for women and weaklings. They moved purposefully towards where the dissenters were disturbing the proceedings.

'You, you! Stop this noise! Leader is speaking! Shut up and listen!' P.K. could have done with a louder and deeper voice, added stature and an air of authority. Lacking all of this, he failed to create even a modest flutter. Driven by genuine pain, dissent and sharp comments continued to fill the air.

'I tell you, you are creating a big disturbance. Leader is upset. Kindly resume your seats!'

Different words, same results. Like his leader, P.K. was not used to insubordination. His eyes bulged, his face turned red, he balled his hands into fists.

'Shut up, I say!'

Again, no sign that he had been heard. Time to bring the heavy artillery into play. He gestured to the Sundarambal Security Services toughs who swung into action.

'Sahib ne bola, chup raho! Nahi to thappad lagega! Suna nahin? Yeh le!'

They spoke no Tamil, the Leader's followers spoke no Hindi and the mutual lack of comprehension soon meant that what started out as simple antipathy soon degenerated into something far worse. Weakened by Rat Kill, the protesters were no match for the toughs. They wilted under the assault and were crushed. Emboldened, and finding the terms of fighting to their liking, the toughs overran the initial pocket of discontent and moved further into the crowd. Big mistake.

Few things arouse a Tamilian's ire more quickly than a Hindi speaker attempting to break his bones with a lathi. Few things fan a Tamilian's ire more than large quantities of alcohol. Untrained they might have been, but they were well-fuelled and had numbers on their side.

P.K.'s success in rounding up followers for the function proved his Waterloo. The fighting was intense but ultimately one-sided. The cream of Sundarambal Security Services had soon been beaten senseless and lay conjoined in a writhing mass with the Rat Kill crowd.

The enraged crowd, looking for something more exciting than a homily on management, found Agarwal's students chattering away in various dialects of Hindi off to one side. The students were taken by surprise. The proceedings up to that point had been conducted in Tamil and a few of them had begun voicing doubts about the wisdom of spending two years in a place where no one spoke Hindi. The director was nowhere to be seen and some others were wondering if the promised MBA admission had just been a ruse to get them to mouth the slogans. They had seen the fighting and wondered just what was going on.

'You! Rascals! Why are you speaking in Hindi?'

'Our Leader is giving Tamil management lessons and you are creating Hindi disturbance!'

'Rascals! Donkeys! Why are you not answering?'

A shower of questions in an alien language, a distinct air of menace, the word Hindi mentioned several times, the response in Hindi slipped out involuntarily.

'Aap jo bol rahe hain hamein samajh mein nahi aa raha hai.'

There was a roar of anger and disbelief from the crowd. These rascals were actually responding to simple questions asked in chaste Tamil with Hindi profanities. Out came sticks, sickles, knives and other tools which constituted the accepted medium of political discourse. The students, quick to spot trouble, ran. The crowd, Leader and function forgotten, chased them.

Their united stand in the face of the AICTE team proved to be an aberration. The faculty meeting continued where it had broken off, and consensus on how to react to their exclusion from the function continued to be elusive. They finally agreed on a silent protest.

'We shall wrap handkerchiefs around our mouths to display our silence.'

'Around our noses also. These fellows are smelling badly.'

'We shall carry white flags to demonstrate our peaceful intent.'

'But they should know why we are doing peaceful silent protest. After all, what is the point of this protest if no one knows the reason for it? The chancellor must see why the faculty is unhappy. He must see what his juniors and sub-juniors are up to.'

'If the chancellor sees our faces, he is liable to take severe disciplining action.'

'We have rights! We are not slaves to his whims and fancies!'

'Whims, fancies and all are truly excellent concepts. Madam, I truly commend you on your knowledge of these concepts.'

'What are you talking about?'

'Madam, as I was saying before your kind interjection, our Leader does not believe in these concepts of whims and fancies. He believes in sticks and lathis.'

'You should have been a poet, professor!'

'Thank you, thank you!'

'It is an important point you have raised, that of our well-being should we undertake this protest. In view of this danger to ourselves, we should reconsider this matter. I am in favour of constituting a sub-committee to give the matter further thought.'

'He is right. If we are recognized, and distinguished management faculty like your good selves are very likely to be recognized, then it is lathi on our backsides for all of us, begging your pardon, madam.'

'I have an idea. Remember the student dramatics last year?'

The desperate students sprinted around the far end of the crowd. Boxed in by a wall on one side, they fought their way around the semi-sensate bodies in their way when they were brought up short.

Marching in a solemn column like priests making

their way down a nave were a group with plastic Gandhi masks strapped on their faces. Dark glasses covered their eyes and handkerchiefs were stuffed up their noses. The lips smiled Gandhiji's familiar smile. The two in front carried a banner which had 'Silent Protest' in both Tamil and English. There were two other banners further down the column. These carried slogans in Tamil.

The students tried backing off but there was too much of a crush behind them. The silent, smiling Gandhis continued their implacable advance. Desperate, bewildered by the day's happenings, aware of the mob on their heels, the students went down on their knees, then into foetal curls to protect themselves from the thrashing that looked imminent.

The ragged fringes of the crowd which had watched the students' sprint with great interest – far more interesting, surely, than the Leader's homily on management and culinary matters – were equally nonplussed by the smiling Gandhis. Dimly aware that the smiling face was familiar, and assuming that the students' hitting the deck represented a form of ritual obeisance, they followed suit. Chalking up brownie points with the almighty made sense in these troubled times. The herd instinct took over and soon large swathes of the crowd had turned away from their leader and were prostrating before the ersatz Gandhis. The mob chasing the students did likewise.

Up on stage, Dr Dr Rakshasan realized that he was getting upstaged. He could see that he was losing his audience to something or someone at the other end. Just what was causing this commotion was unclear.

Tamil politicians do not wear glasses in public. Dr Dr Rakshasan was not an important enough politician to wear dark glasses in public. Myopia ensured that he did not see the processional Gandhis clearly.

He turned to look for P.K.

No P.K.

He looked about him in desperation and saw his wives sweating uncomfortably. He turned to them.

'Di, what is going on there?'

The wives looked at each other in confusion. This wasn't something they had been briefed on and they weren't sure which one of them had been addressed. They looked at their husband for clarification.

He gestured angrily. 'I am asking, what is going on there? Can't any of you see?'

Continued confusion among the wives.

'I am Dr Dr Rakshasan and asking what is going on there. Can't you see that I cannot see and that I am asking you to see?' he shouted.

The mikes picked up his voice and broadcast it to the audience. The silent protest had the audience in thrall, though, and the Leader's lack of vision went unnoticed.

The senior wife, realizing the gravity of the situation, rummaged in her purse and pulled out a pocket telescope that she kept handy for spying on her neighbours. She peered at the protesters.

'They are looking like Gandhi. Silent protest, they are saying.'

'What?'

She rummaged some more and pulled out a 500-rupee note. 'Here, see? Gandhi. Same one exactly.'

'What is this you are saying? That Gandhi died many years ago. Even Indira Gandhi died many years ago.'

'All that I am not knowing but these Gandhis are wearing dark glasses like MGR.'

'What is this silent protest about?'

'Verses from the Thirukkural, I think, but it is far away and I cannot see clearly. Can you buy me a better telescope? Then I can see more clearly and be very helpful to you as well.'

The Sundarambal Security Services squad was equally nonplussed. A few of them had recovered from the beating and were in the process of regrouping. Some were voicing thoughts suggestive of revenge. But their way ahead was blocked by prostrating bodies. Their first instinct was to take advantage of the situation and let loose their lathis on the prone bodies. These bastards deserved nothing less. The sight of the entire crowd showing the deepest respect to the smiling Gandhis made them pause. A few of them instinctively prostrated themselves. The others paused uncertainly for a few minutes before following suit.

The Leader and his wives and the Security Services squad were not the only ones puzzled by the goings on at the far end of the crowd. Poojya Guruji's tryst with South India had been a trying one and now, free at last from his humiliating ceremonial obligations, he was waiting for the ghastly event to run its course. Lost in his thoughts, he had not noticed the Gandhis and the crowd's subsequent distraction. Gradually, though, he realized that the tone of Dr Dr Rakshasan's voice had changed. He looked up to see that the stentorian oratory had given way to a conversation of sorts between wives and husband. One wife was peering through a telescope. Poojya Guruji followed her gaze.

Past a mass of upturned bottoms, past an island of sufferers in the last stages of agony to the distant reaches of the crowd, was a small group, boxed in against a wall, wearing Gandhi masks, dark glasses and handkerchiefs, marching. The vast crowd had gone silent and Dr Dr Rakshasan had gone silent with them.

Poojya Guruji stared at the strange apparition. Like everything in this place it defied sense or logic. Once more he rued coming to this place and wondered when he could make his getaway. He looked around. The masked Gandhis had everyone's attention. The pesky little man with the sword was nowhere in evidence. The thug and his wives, distracted by the masked Gandhis, were carrying on a worried conversation. For the moment at least, he was not part of the crowd's consciousness, and for once he was glad he was not the centre of attention.

The wife was peering through the telescope once more, Dr Dr Rakshasan and his other wives were staring in the same direction, and Poojya Guruji sensed an opportunity. He quietly slid off his seat and, still in a sitting posture, sidled his way off the stage.

He stole another look – the coast looked clear. He was strongly tempted to make a dash for it but held back. A sprinting man in saffron was likely to divert attention from static plastic Gandhis. He made his way around the shamiana towards where he thought his car was. A strange silence hung over the campus and he was conscious of the sound his sandals were making. He slowed down further to silence his shuffle.

There was a sameness to the domed and colonnaded buildings and paths. After a while Poojya Guruji began to sense that he was going around in circles: the car park and his car were nowhere in evidence. His handlers and acolytes had also disappeared. He was sweating profusely by now. He turned another corner – another path with a bright white-domed, colonnaded building – and walked into a group relieving themselves against the columns.

The saffron clothes and beard were recognized immediately: Poojya Guruji's role in the managerial coronation had clearly struck a chord among the lumpen elements. The urinating rabble was keen to make his acquaintance. Poojya Guruji was understandably reluctant to reciprocate. He turned and ran.

Under normal circumstances, it would not have been a fair contest. Years of yoga and Himalayan wanderings along with dietary practices the ancients would have approved of meant that Poojya Guruji was the odds-on favourite in any sort of athletic endeavour, but his saffron robes came in the way of his fulfilling that potential. They got entangled in his legs and he fell. The rabble caught up with him before he had a chance to recover.

It was a brief, unequal, tussle. The rabble quickly relieved Poojya Guruji of his clothes and other belongings. Then they began quarrelling over the spoils. Taking advantage of their preoccupation, Poojya Guruji scrambled to his feet and ran. Unencumbered by clothes, he flew like the wind. This time he found his way to the main gate of the Sundarambal campus and continued his nude sprint on the national highway outside.

Management Lessons from Coimbatore

Overheard at the Delhi Golf Club:

'So there was this massive crowd all suddenly gone silent and prostrating themselves. The boss-man was shouting something but no one was paying any attention. And this lot – the smiling Gandhis with shades and handkerchiefs – had nowhere to go. A wall to one side and a sea of prostrating humanity surrounded them. They shuffled around for a bit and a couple of them were marching in place as though they were at a parade. Then one or two of them decided that they had had enough and picked their way through the prone bodies to clear ground.

'It had been one crazy thing after another and I had to figure out who these chappies were. I tapped one on the shoulder as they came past and, I tell you, there is something completely disconcerting about being stared at by a smiling plastic Gandhi wearing shades and with a handkerchief stuffed up his nose. A few seconds of this and I started feeling quite uneasy. I had decided to give up and walk off when the Gandhi spoke.'

'You are from the AICTE team, right?'

'Yes,' I replied.

'Stephen's quiz team?'

'Yes...how did you know?'

'What do you want now? Can't you see that we are busy?'

That was when some dim measure of recognition seeped in.

'You are...?'

'Yes, yes. I am Professor Thilakavathi. What do you want?'

'I...I see that you are protesting silently... But these masks and glasses?'

'The last time around you thought I was a dog. Now you think I'm Gandhiji.'

'No, no. That's not what I meant. I mean no...yes... the masks...'

'This looks like a silent protest and sounds like a silent protest, but it is actually an exercise in faculty development.'

'I don't really see...'

'I didn't think you would. Woolly-headed bureaucrats sitting in Delhi offices surrounded by sycophants and clerks, what do you know about the world? What do you know about management? What do you know about education? What do you know about anything?'

'That's not fair!'

'What do you think we are doing?'

'I don't really see the connection with faculty development, but...'

'Case proven! You see, you have a very Western and textbook outlook on management. We have our feet on the ground while you drive around in fancy cars. This, Mr Stephens, is an experiment on Gandhian methods in human relations and industrial management. And a successful one. Look at this crowd. You saw what a rowdy lot they were? Look at them now. Now you tell me, is there anything you have read or seen or studied that has managed a lumpen crowd as well as this? Have you even considered the implications for industrial relations and labour productivity? This, Mr Stephens, is how we will beat China. Power comes not from the barrel of a gun but from scientifically tested and validated management ideas. Gandhi, not Mao. And our students shall march forth, torchbearers for these new management ideas forged in the crucible of the real world!'

The envelope was crumpled and scuffed by the time it got to Sambandham. It was something of a miracle that it had actually reached him. It had been addressed to him, care of the Sundarambal Institute of Management.

The Sundarambal Institute of Management no longer existed. The Sundarambal Deemed University did not either.

Following the events described earlier, the campus was shut down pending an inquiry. The inquiry unearthed numerous irregularities. The entire campus had been built on land meant for an afforestation scheme. The management school canteen was found to have toxic levels of rat poison. The duck pond was found to contain two hidden chambers, one containing a large stash of currency notes and the other containing the joint chancellor's personal pornography collection. The chief minister assured agitated members of the legislature that a CID inquiry had been instituted and that the government would be taking over the campus.

One section of the campus was converted to a VVIP helipad. Another now served as a training facility for the canine squad of the state police. Graduates of that programme were used to guard the helipad. Agitated environmentalists who had wanted the area afforested were assured by the government that they would be provided an alternative site for their trees.

The Sundarambal students were accommodated in other colleges. After a hunger strike and several appeals to the chief minister, the faculty were assured positions in various government-run educational institutions. Professor Sambandham ended up as a teacher in a Corporation Primary School in Avinashi. The newspapers and TV channels had gone to town about the chancellor's ceremony and its aftermath, and the Sundarambal connection was something he kept well under wraps. He was rather shocked that the letter had tracked him down.

'It is from Delhi. New Delhi, actually. They are asking me to be co-chairman of this committee.'

Mrs Sambandham, busy in her kitchen, ignored him.

'I'm telling you something important and you are not listening. They are making me co-chairman of this committee on management education. Must be very important. Airfare is even being provided.'

'Are you mad?'

'Look, here is the letter. It is all written here.'

'They are mad, the people who send letters like this to people like you...'

'But...'

'And you must be mad as well.'

'Why?'

'What happened the last time someone made you chairman of a committee?'

'But that was only the director. This is from New Delhi. Indian Government. Ministry of Human Resources Development.'

'You are a fool. You never learn. Just like last time some silly woman will make a fool of you. Stick to your teaching. No more committee business for you.'

'But...'

'Show me that letter.'

He handed it over. She looked it over.

'Read it to me. All this English I am not understanding.'

Sambandham translated as he read.

Dear Professor Sambandham,

I am pleased to invite you to join the Committee on Post-Graduate Management Education set up by the Ministry of Human Resource Development as the Co-Chairperson.

The Committee has been tasked with making actionable suggestions for improving management education at the post-graduate level. Specifically:

1. The Committee will look into the relevance of existing management curricula in view of current management practices.
2. The Committee will look into the practice of using textbooks and case studies with an American orientation. The desirability of teaching American practices and values in light of the recent global developments will also be studied.
3. The Committee will study the suggestions made by Prof. Henry Mintzberg and come up with methods to incorporate them into curricula while keeping the Indian management ethos in mind.
4. The Committee will consider innovative methods to upgrade faculty capabilities. The role of team-building activities and role-playing exercises might be considered in this regard.
5. The Committee will look into ways of inculcating social responsibility, ethics and awareness of the environment in management students. The role of team-building activities and role-playing exercises might be considered in this regard.

Professor Thilakavathi of the Sundarambal Institute of Management has been invited to be your Co-Chairperson in this Committee. While you would convene the groups discussing items 3 and 5 as elaborated above, Professor Thilakavathi would convene the group discussing item 4.

You would jointly convene the groups discussing items 1 and 2.

The Committee shall include the Directors of the Indian Institutes of Management at Ahmedabad, Bangalore and Kolkata, the Secretary in the Ministry of Human Resource Development, the Director of AICTE and a representative from the PMO. The Committee is empowered to convene sub-committees to study specific issues in depth. The Ministry of Human Resource Development shall establish a secretariat headed by a Joint Secretary to assist the Committee in its deliberations.

Meetings of the Committee shall be held in New Delhi. Business class airfare, a per diem payment of Rs 5,000 and suitable accommodation shall be provided to all committee members attending the meetings.
Kindly convey your acceptance to the undersigned.

Yours sincerely,
Rajesh K. Ranjan
Secretary
Ministry of Human Resource Development

There was a minute or two of silence.

Mrs Sambandham finally spoke. She was in the grip of strong emotions and the words came out with difficulty. 'It is all a trick.'

'But look. This is official stationary. New Delhi government stationary. Rubber stamp and signature even. See, undersigned has even signed the letter.'

'I'm telling you, it is a trick. By that woman Thilakavathi. First, she is calling you home pretending that her scooter is not working. Now she is sending you letters like this. See, her name is on the letter. All these tricks only to seduce you.'

'But government only is offering her this position...'

'Nonsense! Why would any government want to offer her any position? She is a stupid woman, not even fit for teaching in that college. Why they gave her a job, God only knows. You are also a fool, thinking that this is a real letter and that government is giving that stupid woman the same position as you.'

'She has only one item, they are giving me two items. Look it says that here...'

'One item, two items. See, she is a very clever woman. She has written this letter very cleverly giving you two items and herself only one item and like a fool you think you are very clever and all.'

'But...'

'I am telling you one last time this is a trick by that scoundrel rascal woman. She will say committee this committee that, item this item that, and call you to her house. And you, like a fool, will go there and...and...I cannot even speak what all I am thinking...terrible things she will do. Nothing doing. Luckily I have caught her trick this time.'

Mrs Sambandham tore up the letter with firm flicks of her wrist until it was in shreds.

'Next time she tries some trick, you better tell me. Now you go back to that school and teach.'

Sambandham could only nod dumbly.

Acknowledgements

Thanks to Nandita Aggarwal for helping me tighten and structure this story better.

To Amish Raj Mulmi and Shivmeet Deol for editing the manuscript.

To Punya for help and advice on my writing career.

To Chitra and Krishna for all the years of conversation at the beach.

Above all, to Ambika and Vishwanath for keeping my feet on the ground, for their support, love and encouragement.